D0775714

# Hard and Ruthless 2

Von Diesel

**Lock Down Publications and Ca$h**
**Presents**
# Hard and Ruthless 2
### A Novel by *Von Diesel*

**Lock Down Publications**
P.O. Box 944
Stockbridge, Ga 30281
www.lockdownpublications.com

Copyright 2021 by Von Diesel
Hard and Ruthless 2

All rights reserved. No part of this book may be reproduced in any form or by electronic or mechanical means, including information storage and retrieval systems without permission in writing from the publisher, except by a reviewer who may quote brief passages in review.
First Edition May 2021
Printed in the United States of America

*This is a work of fiction. Names, characters, places, and incidents either are products of the author's imagination or are used fictitiously. Any similarity to actual events or locales or persons, living or dead, is entirely coincidental.*

**Lock Down Publications**
**Like our page on Facebook: Lock Down Publications @**
www.facebook.com/lockdownpublications.ldp
Cover design and layout by: **Dynasty Cover Me**
Book interior design by: **Shawn Walker**
Edited by: **Leondra Williams**

# Stay Connected with Us!

Text **LOCKDOWN** to 22828 to stay up-to-date with new releases, sneak peaks, contests and more…

Thank you!

# Submission Guideline.

Submit the first three chapters of your completed manuscript to ldpsubmissions@gmail.com, subject line: Your book's title. The manuscript must be in a .doc file and sent as an attachment. Document should be in Times New Roman, double spaced and in size 12 font. Also, provide your synopsis and full contact information. If sending multiple submissions, they must each be in a separate email.

Have a story but no way to send it electronically? You can still submit to LDP/Ca$h Presents. Send in the first three chapters, written or typed, of your completed manuscript to:

LDP: Submissions Dept
P.O. Box 944
Stockbridge, Ga 30281

*DO NOT send original manuscript. Must be a duplicate.*

Provide your synopsis and a cover letter containing your full contact information.

Thanks for considering LDP and Ca$h Presents.

Von Diesel

## Chapter One

As Swerve fought for another breath, thoughts of Yoshi and his two sons invaded his mind, and then Rhapsodee. How could he leave without even apologizing for the damage that he caused to the both of them? How could he leave without even saying goodbye? Swerve saw a white light and then everything went black.

It was Cadillac Dave's turn for the shower. As he approached, he saw a lifeless body laying down on the floor surrounded by a pool of blood.

"Man down! Somebody help," yelled Cadillac Dave.

As the guards approached the scene and saw the body and the pool of blood, they immediately called for help and instructed everyone to go to their assigned cells.

"Alright everybody, in your cells now! I don't know which one of you fucktards are responsible for what just happened to this here fella, but when I find out the bitch ass that did it, you gonna be doing the rest of your time up under this got damn jail," spat the fat redneck lieutenant.

"Yo man, c'mon. We gotta get the fuck up outta here," said J'Shon.

As Cadillac Dave neared his cell, he noticed that the young gentleman was in tow behind him.

"Yo, don't shut the door, they just assigned me to that cell," ordered J'Shon.

As soon as Cadillac Dave entered his cell, he noticed that ol' dude now occupied his space. The guards had wasted no time putting someone in the room with him.

"You're on my bunk," Cadillac Dave said as he looked at the man in frustration. The man made no effort to move. Cadillac Dave wasn't in the mood for muthafuckas and their attitudes. He was already dealing with his case as well as someone to take his anger out on. He walked over to his new cell mate and snatched the sandwich he was eating out of his hand.

"Why you all up in my shit? I put my shit where the guard told me to," the man said.

"And now I'm telling you to put it somewhere else," Cadillac Dave said. He wouldn't normally make such a big deal out of things, but he didn't feel like allowing ol' boy to think he could come up in there running shit.

He tossed the sandwich onto the adjacent bunk. A few awkward seconds ticked by before the man gave in.

"I saw you on the news and I know what happened with your case. That shit was fucked up. That's the only reason why I ain't all up in your ass right now," the man said.

Cadillac Dave found laughter for the first time in days. "Oddly enough, it's the only reason I'm all in yours right now."

They had come to an understanding without coming to blows and Cadillac Dave appreciated it.

## Chapter Two

Bobby B felt it would be best to stay at a hotel for a few days, at least until he got his head right. He figured if the cops knew where E-Love's cash spots were, then nine times outta ten, they knew where all of them were.

E-Love hadn't missed a beat when it came down to niggas being disloyal in his pack, but most of the time D'Lamar was the one who always peeped their game.

Lately E-Love had been handy with the steel, sending shots to niggas domes who had damn near lost their lives in an attempt to save his.

For some odd reason, Bobby B was thinking that D'Lamar had something to do with the stash spot being raided and him going to jail. He wouldn't tell E-Love of his suspicions concerning D'Lamar until he could back them up.

He was broken out of his thoughts when a call from E-Love came through.

"Yo whaddup B?"

"What up, my nigga? How's family life treating you?"

"Life is good. Life is good. It's time to re-up. I know you probably all spooked and shit about them blues running up in the spot, so I'ma let you chill for a minute and see if D'Lamar can take this ride wit' a nigga to Miami," spat E-Love.

"D'Lamar? Since when you start letting that nigga ride dirty wit' you? Nah man, I can't let you go out like that. What time we heading out?"

E-Love looked down at his watch and said, "I wanna get outta' here within the next hour. You sure you down wit' it?"

"Hell yeah my nigga! Dade County, here we come."

Von Diesel

## Chapter Three

Leah was on cloud nine. She had married the man of her dreams and had given him a set of twins. Her and E-Love had their share of problems but had managed to overcome them. Leah was still feeling the shame of almost being intimate with E-Love's father. Had the shoe been on the other foot, she wouldn't have ever forgiven E-Love had he pulled up on her mother.

From time to time she could still smell Sebastian's Humme by Dior cologne. It was damned near breathtaking. What if her and Sebastian had taken that next step to intimacy and later found out he was E-Love's father?

"Hey baby, I'm about to dip. I'm gonna be out of town for a couple of days. I asked my moms to stop by to see if you needed any help with the twins. I hope you didn't mind," said E-Love.

"Thank you, babe. Where exactly are you going?" asked Leah.

"Miami, but it's gonna be a quick turnaround as usual," he explained.

"Baby please be careful. You know the game better that I do. You know I don't like jumping to any conclusions, but I hope you don't plan on doing this for the rest of your life. I need you and so do the twins, and if anything ever happened to you…"

"Shhh…It won't! Nothing is gonna happen to me. I'm gonna be around for a long time. This will be over soon, I promise baby," insured E-Love.

He kissed his queen and his twins and headed for the door.

Leah didn't know what to do with herself. She hadn't had a girl's night out since she had the twins. She decided to call her all girl gang for a night out on the town. Leah picked up her iPhone and called Rhapsodee.

"Uh, look who's calling. What's up girl and how's my baby cousins doing?" asked Rhapsodee.

"We doing just fine. Just thought we could get together tomorrow night for a drink or something."

"Shid…I don't see why not. Let me hit up Princess and Twin and I'll text you with the details. I love you cuz," said Rhapsodee.

"Love you too."

Leah called her mother-in-law to confirm that she had a babysitter for Saturday night. Her mother-in-law confirmed and from there it was a go. She looked in the mirror at her Coca-Cola bottle figure and asked herself, "What should I wear?"

## Chapter Four

The guards rolled Swerve down the hall, practically running toward the infirmary as the doctor administered CPR. Swerve had lost so much blood and his blood pressure was so low that the doctor feared it may be too late. She had seen many things but never had seen such a handsome man like the one laying before her so lifeless. Swerve's life was at stake. The doctor only prayed that she could keep Swerve stable until the ambulance arrived. Healthcare in the prison or jail system wasn't equipped for this type of emergency and the doctor hoped that today wouldn't be the day that a prisoner died on her watch.

Just as the doctor finished praying, the EMTs walked in and wheeled Swerve directly to the ambulance and sped away.

The fat red-neck lieutenant grabbed Swerve's jail records and rushed out of the room.

"Wait for me," said the doctor.

"Shit, where's his medical records?" asked the lieutenant.

"I'll get them, just pull the car around to the front entrance."

The doctor hurriedly grabbed Swerve's medical records and rushed to the front entrance. As she spotted the lieutenant, she jumped in the car and they drove away.

"So, lieutenant, this young man has only been locked away for two weeks now. What could he have done that was so bad for someone to wanna damn near kill him?" the doctor asked.

"I don't know. We booked him in on first degree murder, it could have been a relative of his victim on some get back type of shit. It happens here all the time, but this is the first time it's actually happened in our jail," explained the lieutenant.

"Wow, and he's so young to be having all of this drama in his life. His mother must be worried sick about him."

"From the looks of his jail records, his mother is deceased. Only next of kin is his wife. You wanna give her a call?

"Sure," said the doctor.

She grabbed her cell phone and dialed the emergency contact on file.

"Yes, this is Doctor Monet at Fulton County Jail. I'm calling in reference to your husband, Mr. James St. John. I hate to be the bearer of bad news, but your husband was stabbed today. He's being transferred to Grady Hospital. You are more than welcomed to come if you would like. Me and Lieutenant Walters will be in the waiting room," explained the doctor.

"Ma'am, thanks for calling, but Rhapsodee is no longer Mr. St. John's wife. See, she belongs to me now. As far as we're concerned the son of a bitch can rot in hell. Maybe now he can join his low life ass mammy. Oh doc, I almost forgot...DON'T CALL HERE AGAIN!" ordered Black.

She had never heard such harsh words in all of her life. What could Swerve have done to make his wife leave him for another man. She didn't know, but she would soon find out.

"So, what did his wife say?" asked the lieutenant.

"Oh, it was the answering service, hopefully she will get the message," said the doctor.

## Chapter Five

Rhapsodee was enjoying her man just as Leah had instructed her to do. While looking at her engagement ring, she thought back to her marriage with Swerve and began to cry. She never thought in a million years that Swerve would have disrespected and dishonored her the way that he did. Hearing of Swerve's tragedy brought a relief upon her, but deep down inside she still loved him. She could have understood why she would have stabbed him but couldn't understand why someone else would beat her to the punch. Their marriage had been on the rocks ever since she caught him getting his dick sucked by his estranged side piece. She did everything that a good wife was supposed to do, but Swerve didn't know how to appreciate any of that. She closed her eyes and thanked God for sending Black her way and for not planting any of Swerve's seeds inside of her. She was interrupted by the soft kisses that Black was planting on her neck.

"So that nigga finally got a taste of sweet revenge," said Black.

"I hate to say it, but lucky for him that someone in jail stabbed him. I was on the verge of quirking out on his ass, and God knows that I couldn't have spent the rest of my life in prison over that nothing ass muthafucka," said Rhapsodee.

"Maybe they'll find the person responsible for stabbing him. If they do, let's send him a thank you card," Black replied.

Deep down inside Rhapsodee couldn't stomach Black saying harsh words about Swerve. Swerve was a muthafucka, but he was still her husband. Hearing Black disrespect him didn't quite settle well with her, so she quickly changed the subject.

"So, can we get back to the part when you were kissing me on my neck?" cooed Rhapsodee.

Black was stroking his dick in a long, slow motion, and she would be damned if she didn't want some of it. She might as well get the best nut of her life. The fact that his dick curved upward and to the left was definitely a plus. It was heavy too. She knew for sure he would be knocking against her g-spot. Her pussy was looking forward to it.

Walking over to the bed, she waited until his dick was damn near throbbing. Through his half-closed eyes, he watched her give him head while he finger fucked her pussy and smacked her on her ass. She wondered for a second if his fingers felt better than his manhood, but she lost that thought when he guided her to sit down on the head of his dick. Once she slid down his pole, she felt that crooked dick feeling around for her g-spot. She bounced and wiggled on that muthafucka until he tickled her fancy. A gush of her sweet juices started to flow down the sides of his dick.

"Damn baby, all of this good dick belongs to you. Only you. Don't stop! Just keep riding. I want you to cream all over this big black dick."

Rhapsodee slowly eased up from Black's magic stick and gripped it with her muscles. The feeling made Black scream damn near to the top of his lungs. He didn't want Rhapsodee to know how good it felt for her to be in control, so he instructed her to lay flat on her back. He went to his side drawer of his nightstand and pulled out two sets of handcuffs and put the key around his chain. He inserted a cuff on each leg and snapped them securely around the bottom bed posts seeing a full view of Rhapsodee's juicy pussy laid slap the fuck open. He pulled up a chair and pulled her ass to the end of the bed as far as it would go and devoured her pussy as if it was his last meal. Rhapsodee squirmed, moaned and squirted all up in Black's face like never before. Seeing that Rhapsodee's chest was going up and down as if she was having convulsions, Black sucked her clit one last time and left it swollen and purple. He uncuffed her legs, laid her on her stomach, then went ape shit inside of her sugar walls. Rhapsodee screamed out in agony as Black let out a loud roar and nutted inside of her. Being that Rhapsodee was too sore to move, he covered her up with a soft plush blanket, and then fell asleep beside her.

## Chapter Six

A light rap on the cell door awoke Cadillac Dave as the C.O. told him to get ready for court. He brushed his teeth, washed his face and took his morning piss just as the door was opening.

"Yo man, good luck in court," spat J'Shon.

"Preciate it, young blood," replied Cadillac Dave as he exited the door.

His stomach was in knots as he entered the courtroom and sat at the defendant's table with his lawyer. He didn't know if it was anxiety, or the bubble guts, but he surely felt sick. Minutes later, the prosecutor came and sat across from him at his table. Then came the judge.

He took a deep breath as the prosecution began.

"Your honor, we would like to request a continuance. Our key witness was killed in the line of duty. Sharon Jackson-Perez, the lead detective on this case, had gathered an enormous amount of evidence and tapes that led to the indictment of Mr. David Jerome Brewer, aka Cadillac Dave. Without her here to testify, the prosecution needs a little more time to develop a stronger case."

His attorney stood up to speak. "Your Honor, the defense would like to request a bond until the next trial date."

"Continuance granted. Bond set at one hundred thousand dollars," said the judge.

As Cadillac Dave entered back into his cell, he couldn't help but smile. He had been down for damn near thirty days without a bond. In a matter of time, he would be back out in the sunshine grinding hard and knee deep in some pussy. "That nigga that I found in the shower, was the one who was booked in for her murder. I saw that shit on TV. Damn, that nigga gone be fucked if he lives. He killed a fuckin' cop. It's all coming together now," thought Cadillac Dave.

He was broken out of his chain of thought when J'Shon interrupted him.

"So, you gettin' out or what?" asked J'Shon.

"Yeah man, they gave me a bond. I'm out this bitch!"

"Yeah, I'm out this bitch too. They gave me 24 hours for public intoxication. We might bounce out this bitch at the same damn time," spat J'Shon.

"Shid...I'm tryin' to get me some pussy. You ever heard of the Sugar Shak," asked Cadillac Dave.

"Yeah, what about it?" asked J'Shon.

"Let's hit it up. It be some fine ass bitches up in that joint. Shid... T.I., Thug, Jeezy... All them niggas gone be performing and poppin' bottles tonight. You wit' me?"

"Hell yeah," spat J'Shon.

"Just as Cadillac Dave scribbled his contact info down for J'Shon, the both of them were released.

Money that he had saved up for emergencies was just enough for him to make bond.

## Chapter Seven

When Rhapsodee had finally awakened, she rolled over to an empty side of the bed. She reached over to the nightstand and picked up her iPhone. There was a message from Black saying that he had to pick Sosa up from the airport and that he had to handle some business. Rhapsodee was furious, but her pussy was all smiles. Black had given her some bomb ass sex the night before. He surprised her with the handcuffs. She had no way to maneuver her body...only her mind. She knew that she had that come back pussy and she was sure Black was whipped. The thought of him taking Swerve's place let her know that she could love again. Rhapsodee never put all of her trust in any man, and Swerve pulling his lil' stunts with his hoe ass bitches didn't help the situation either. Reflecting back on their past, she knew that Swerve really loved her. Putting up with his bullshit had gotten the best of her. She was damn near in forgive mode had she not found out that he had a son and a newborn son with his side piece Yoshi. She decided to get up, shower and head off to the nail shop and beauty salon for some much-needed pampering. She picked up the phone and called Leah.

"Hey cuz, what's poppin?"

"Not too much. Did you and the crew decide where we're going tonight?" Leah asked.

"Oh yeah, I almost forget. We decided on hittin' up the Sugar Shak," said Rhapsodee.

"Girl, are you serious? I haven't been there in years. Who's opening the joint up tonight?" asked Leah.

"Just the locals, T.I., Young Thug, Lil Boosie.

"So, you gonna pick me up or what?" asked Leah.

"I guess we can carpool. Ten-thirty okay?"

"That gives me plenty of time," said Leah.

"Alright cuz, see you later."

As they ended their call, Rhapsodee jumped up from her bed, showered and headed out.

Von Diesel

## Chapter Eight

E-Love and Bobby B had finally made it to Miami. Coming from Atlanta was a fuckin' hump, but the payout was gonna be more than worth the trip. E-Love had been dealing with Red-Bean over in Liberty City for what seemed like a decade. His supply was always pure and uncut just like he liked it. Red-Bean was strictly business and that's just the way E-Love intended to keep it.

"A'ight my nigga, we here. Wake yo tired ass up," spat E-Love.

"Damn we got here quick as fuck," said Bobby B.

"Yeah, we did. It be like that when yo' ass be sleep the whole fucking time, not helping a nigga drive," said E-Love.

Bobby B grabbed the duffel back with the cash inside and secured his 9mm in the waist of his Red Monkey jeans. E-Love threw on his tinted-out Ray bans and secured his Smith and Wesson in place as well. As they exited E-Love's Yukon all eyes were on them as they walked through the gate. They were greeted by one of Red-Beans viscous ass pit bulls.

"No need to be frightened gentlemen, come on in," instructed Red-Bean.

"No need to be frightened? Shid... I ain't never seen a pit bull that won't bite the shit outta' muthafucka," said E-Love.

"Only if she smells some bullshit. But in this instance, I think all is well. What brings you fellas to Dade County?" asked Red-Bean.

"Business as usual. I'm looking to get my hands on about twenty-five keys, think you can handle that for me?" asked E-Love.

Red-Bean let out a slight chuckle and replied, "That's small change in this city. I thought guys of your caliber would be looking for more."

"Twenty-five keys is all I can afford right now. A nigga wishing they could wear your status on their sleeve one day," replied E-Love.

"Well since you said it like that, Mario...bring the fellas what they're asking for," ordered Red-Bean.

"Just so we on the same page, you know it's $29,000 for each key, so you do the math," said Red-Bean.

"Bet, spat E-Love. It's all in the bag."

"Count it up, and if it's all there, you gentlemen can take your product and be on your way."

"It's all there, boss," said Mario.

"Alright gentlemen, Mario says it's all there. You fellas have a safe trip back to the A," instructed Red-Bean.

E-Love and Bobby B grabbed the duffel bag with the drugs secured inside and made their exit through the front door. Once outside E-Love took off his shades and blew out a sigh of relief.

"Yo man, that nigga deadly," spat Bobby B.

"I know, he a piece of work, but he the only connect I got right now. Hopefully we should be at retirement status in a couple more months, and then we'll never have to make this trip again," said E-Love.

"Word?" asked Bobby B.

"Word, my nigga," spat E-Love.

As they hopped in the Yukon, E-Love threw in Notorious B.I.G.'s *Juicy* in the cd player and then sped away.

"Yo, E man, I been wanting to talk to you about that sucka ass D'Lamar," said Bobby B.

"What about him?" asked E-Love.

## Chapter Nine

The four of them were back together again. It had been a while since they hit the club together, so of course, they had to represent. Rhapsodee was dressed in an all-black halter top catsuit by Versace. She wore her hair straight, and it flowed nicely down her back. She applied a glitter gloss to her lips, along with an earth tone eyeshadow that complimented her slanted eyes. After all of her last-minute primping, she slid her freshly pedicured feet into her Fendi sandals and was ready for what the fuck ever.

"Princess was dressed a little too conservatively for Rhapsodee's taste, in a knee-length Chanel skirt with a button up blouse by Donna Karan. Sister girl needed some serious help.

"Uh, hell no! You ain't going with me looking like that. We going to a club, not a fucking job interview," Rhapsodee spat.

"I know, but I didn't have anything else to wear," Princess whined.

Rhapsodee dug down into her bag and pulled out a fitted little dress by Gucci. "Here. Put this on," she said, throwing it at Princess.

The dress was a little too short and a little too sexy for Princess, but she had no other choice in the matter, so she just decided to roll with it. Rhapsodee took care of her hair and makeup and Princess threw on some stiletto mid-calf boots from Jimmy Choo to at least hide some of her legs.

Twin arrived at a quarter past eleven. She was looking cute as well, wearing a black-and-white sheer shirt that hung off her left shoulder, black stretch boot cut pants, and a pair of heels. She wasn't really into all that name brand shit. To her, it was the person that made the clothes, not the other way around. So, while chicks were out there trying to keep up with the Kardashians, spending three or four hundred for an outfit, Twin's cost about seventy bucks and she looked good.

Leah walked in sporting a pair of stretch fitted True Religion Jeans, a tight fitted True Religion tee, and a pair of wheat Timberland heel boots. She had her hair slick back into a long straight ponytail that hung to the middle of her back and her makeup was on fleek.

The girls made it to the Sugar Shak around midnight. They headed straight to the bar. The club was kinda empty at first, but it didn't take long for it to fill up.

The Sugar Shak was also a well-known spot for the celebrities. That particular night, Young Thug, T.I., Gucci Mane and Rich Homie Quan were up in there poppin' bottles.

Twin, of course being the diva, she only knew how to be, wanted nothing less than VIP status, plus she wanted T.I. to notice her and how good she looked in her shimmering apparel.

She started by making eye contact with one of the bouncers in front of the velvet ropes. His arms were folded, and he didn't seem to pay her much attention.

She walked over to him and bluntly asked," Ahhh, can you let me and my girls through, please?"

Without even looking down at her, he replied," Nah shorty, I can't."

"Come on. I said please. I'll give you my number," Twin said with a flirtatious smile.

He gave her a dirty ass look. Disappointed and bothered by the bouncer's rejection, Twin stormed off and headed back over to Rhapsodee, Leah and Princess, who stood holding their drinks, waiting patiently for her to signal them over to the VIP.

"That muthafucka' gotta be gay," she yelled out to them over the loud music.

"Or maybe you lost your touch." Rhapsodee laughed at her snide remark.

"Never that." Twin didn't find the humor at all.

"Oh, come on, you guys. Let's just have some fun." Leah was the mediator as usual.

"Yeah, lets." Princess rolled her eyes.

"Rhapsodee, just give me my drink. You, Leah, and Princess go have fun. I'ma go stand over there." Twin said, pointing toward the VIP section.

"You sure?" asked Leah.

"Yeeesss, Go!" Twin yelled as she headed back over the ropes. She was certain she'd get up in VIP.

The DJ was putting it down with the music. The fellas were hawking the females like vultures. It didn't take long for Princess, Rhapsodee and Leah to find dance partners.

Twin sipped on her drink and checked out the scene carefully. Suddenly, she felt a tap on her shoulder. Slowly she turned to her left, and there stood a six-foot-four, nicely built, caramel brother with hazel eyes.

"What's your name shorty?" he asked with a killer smile. Jackpot bells went off in Twin's head when she looked down and saw he was standing on the other side of the ropes in VIP, where she needed to be. She smiled at him, damn near showing all her pearly whites.

"Twin."

"Twin?" he repeated.

"Uh-huh."

"That's nice. It's different."

Twin smiled again, moving seductively to the music and taking a sip from her glass.

"What you drinking?"

"Cotton-Candy Vodka," she replied in a sexy but girlish kind of tone.

"Oh word. So why don't you come chill with me and have another one."

She smiled some more. "Okay."

"Yo dude let shorty through," he said to the bouncer.

Twin gave the bouncer a mean "You should've let me through the first time look" as he shook his head and reluctantly unhooked the rope to let her through. She walked over to her new friends table, and he introduced her to his new partner and two girls that looked like video hoes with all of their assets hanging out.

"Okay, I know their names, but I don't know yours," she said. He gave her a dumbfounded look, like she was supposed to know who he was.

"That's cause you ain't ask."

"I'm asking you now," Twin replied.

"Dave."

"Cadillac Dave."

"Oh, okay!"

The two of them hit it off so well that she forgot all about the celebs and her girls. Cadillac Dave entertained her with his conversations, jokes, and plenty of Cotton-Candy Vodka.

Twin didn't allow her thoughts of Cadillac Dave to soak her panties. On a scale of one to ten, she'd rated him a ten. A big nigga like him had to be equipped.

"Twin!" Rhapsodee was standing next to the security guard.

"Yo, is that your friend calling you?" Cadillac Dave asked.

"Yeah, that's one of them," she said, getting up to see what Rhapsodee wanted.

"Nah, hold up a minute!" Cadillac Dave pulled Twin back down in the seat. "Yo, homie, he called out to the bouncer. Let her through."

"Sorry man, I can't let no more through right now," the bouncer replied.

"That's all right. Let me just go see what she wants okay?" Twin stated to Cadillac Dave as she got up and walked over to Rhapsodee.

"What up girl?" asked Twin.

"Nothing, but we ready to go."

"Already?" Twin said, looking down at her diamond face Rolie, which only read three a.m.

"Yeah, I'm tired, and I think Princess had too much to drink."

Twin sucked her teeth and let out a hard sight. "Okay, just give me five minutes."

"All right. We'll be waiting by the exit. "Hold up! Is that Swerve's ass with his arm wrapped around one of those stripper bitches?" asked Rhapsodee.

Now how in the fuck is that Swerve, when his ass laid up in Grady Hospital? I'm starting to think your ass is the one who's had too much to drink.

Twin walked back over to Cadillac Dave with an agitated look on her face.

"What's up?" he asked.

"Nothing. I should've driven my own car, that's all, but since I didn't, I have to go now."

"Ahhh, come on. You can't be serious. Our vibe is too good for you to go now."

"Yeah, but my girls are ready now."

"So then let them go and I'll take you home."

The offer sounded good, but Twin didn't want to seem too thirsty. Besides, the last time she was with a guy, she ended up with a bullet in her chest, so it was best that she played it safe.

"Nah, I'm gonna go, but why don't you take my number?"

"Oh, no doubt. Hold up. Let me put it in my phone," Cadillac Dave said. "Okay now, what is it?"

Twin recited her number while he punched the keys on his phone and then repeated them back to her. "A'ight sexy, I'ma holla at you."

Twin blushed as she said goodnight.

"Damn these bitches get on my nerves," she mumbled under her breath, making her way to the exit.

Von Diesel

## Chapter Ten

"What about D'Lamar?" Asked E-Love.

"Man, that nigga on some shady shit. I been checking out the way that cat been moving. He getting to be real reckless with his shit. Before Moon got his cradle rocked, he told me how D'Lamar be eyeing Leah. He told me how that nigga was on some shiesty shit. Then he come calling you up saying ole' boy needed to be taught a lesson. He knew that if he said it, you believed it. Then right before the stash spot got raided, I saw that nigga car rolling through the hood. I knew some shit was up, so I went and hid all the money and the majority of the drugs in the safe spot, then outta nowhere them boys in blue banging on the door and shit. Good thing I only had a couple joints in that muthafucka. If you noticed, that nigga ain't been calling like he used to. And when you don't hear from D'Lamar, something ain't right."

"You right, my nigga. Now that you've mentioned it, nigga been acting real shady tho fa real," spat E-Love.

"Man, pull over at that gas station right there. Nigga gotta piss," spat Bobby B.

"Yeah, I'ma fill this bitch up."

As soon as E-Love pulled off a couple of cop cars got in tow behind him. He made sure he wasn't swerving or speeding. Five minutes down the road, the cop threw on his siren.

"Man, I can't believe this shit!' E-Love said as he pulled over. With a scowl look on his face, he watched as them niggas exited their cars with their hands on their weapons. One moved to Bobby B's side and the other one, his way.

When that muthafucka knocked on E-Love's window, he hit the switch with his left hand and placed his right hand on the steering wheel so he could see. "How can I help you officer?"

"License and registration please."

*Damn, this shit bout to blow up* Bobby B thought.

"Can you boys step outside of the vehicle with your hands up?" asked the officer. They cuffed the both of them and placed them in the back of the cop car while they searched E-Love's truck.

Ten minutes later, an unmarked car arrived on the scene and the cops started unloading the drugs out of E-Love's truck into the back of the other vehicle, and it immediately sped away.

The officers then walked over to E-Love and Bobby and said, "I see you two boys from the ATL, we left five of the keys in your truck as evidence and we took the other twenty off your hands, for your troubles. Just consider today your lucky day fellas."

E-Love watched his vehicle being towed as the cop hauled him and Bobby B off to jail.

## Chapter Eleven

Rhapsodee awoke with a throbbing headache from drinking the night before. When she got home, Black wasn't there, nor had he even attempted to call. She messaged him several times but never received any type of response. She was worried sick. As she looked in the medicine cabinet to retrieve some Advil for her migraine, she noticed that Swerve's cologne was still living there. She sprayed a dab of it in the air just to see if she could still recall his smell. Tears began to swell in her eyes. She wondered how she could be so mean and inconsiderate. She had allowed Black to consume her thoughts and get into her head about her husband. She loved Swerve, but she was in love with Black. She thought about Black's proposal but could never foresee being his wife because Swerve wouldn't sign the divorce papers. Maybe attempting to marry Black was too soon. Was she moving too fast? Debating whether or not to check on her husband was troubling her mind. Rhapsodee couldn't take not seeing him. She showered and got dressed.

Rhapsodee wasted no time getting to the hospital. Doing a hundred miles per hour on the expressway. Under any other circumstances, she would have been car sick from that type of speed, but this time was different.

"Hurry, Rhapsodee, hurry," she hollered.

She arrived at the hospital in ten minutes flat. She pulled up to the front of the emergency entrance, hopped out of the car and rushed through the emergency waiting room.

"Ma'am, excuse me. You can't park there," said the security guard.

Rhapsodee pushed past the guard. Right now, her only concern was her husband and finding out about his condition. Then, she wanted the bastard that was responsible for trying to kill him.

"Excuse me, miss. I'm looking for my husband, James St. John. He was stabbed and brought in by ambulance a couple of days ago. Can you tell me where to find him please?" Rhapsodee begged.

The lady punched Swerve's name into the computer and directed her to the intensive care unit. Once she reached ICU, she still had to follow the same procedure.

"Excuse me. I was told that I could find my husband here. His name is James St. John. He's thirty-six years old and he was stabbed over in Fulton County Jail," this time getting even more impatient and hoping she could assist her. Before the nurse could answer any questions, the doctor walked up.

"Excuse me, I'm Doctor Seville. Did I overhear you asking about a young man that was stabbed? Are you next of kin?"

"Yes, I am. I'm his wife. Is he okay, doctor?" Rhapsodee asked.

"Come with me please. It's been a long morning." Doctor Seville let out a sigh as the both of them began walking down the corridor. "Your husband was stabbed in his throat. When he was brought in, he had already lost an enormous amount of blood. We had to rush him into surgery right away. His heart rate was fading fast, and we were without a doubt going to lose him. I had no choice but to authorize an emergency transfusion to get his heart to start pumping again."

Rhapsodee's jaw dropped.

"As of now, your husband's condition is still critical. He's in a coma, and due to his injuries, he's on a respirator. Your husband is definitely a fighter, and I strongly believe he will pull through this."

## Chapter Twelve

Black knew that Rhapsodee would go ape shit once he returned her call. Not coming home wasn't something that he wouldn't have ever imagined doing. Once he picked Sosa up from the airport and dropping off Cadillac Dave some clothes at the hotel, he and Sosa decided to ride to New Orleans to speak with one of his father's connects. He saw where Rhapsodee had called several times and left millions of texts. He tried calling her, but for some odd reason the call was saying that she had traveled outside of the calling area.

Being that they were on the same plan, he accessed the find my iPhone app to see her location. What he saw made him want to roll up on her ass and do a Rambo, but instead he used that as his excuse for him not going home again tonight. The bitch had the nerve to be posted up at Grady Hospital visiting that nigga Swerve. *How she gonna play him?* He was literally using the bitch at first so he could keep tabs with that nigga, but when she threw that sweet lil' pussy of hers on him...he couldn't help but take shit to another level.

He followed her to the Wal-Mart that day, just to see how the bitch rolled. Getting a piece of ass was all he intended, but shit took a wrong turn. He let his feelings get the best of him.

Swerve didn't know that he was sent to rob him of his life savings. He had skipped town with the insurance money from his mother's death. His father had got into a little run-in with the Haitians. He had purchased fifty keys on credit but didn't have the money like he promised. His dad was going to use the insurance money to pay the Haitians' off, but Swerve took off with it. Black, being the jackass that he was, and black sheep of the family was chosen by his father to find Swerve and compensate his funds. That's right, Swerve is Black's half-brother. Fucking this niggas wife was right up his alley. Last time he saw that nigga they were about six-year-old. Swerve didn't recognize who Black was when he popped up with E-Love that day. Nigga always thought that he was the only son. Black was always hiding in the cut by his father since he and his mother only had a one-night stand. His moms used to be a prostitute back in the day, and his sperm donor was one of her customers. His dad never told him he was the type of cat to buy pussy, but the neighborhood did.

## Chapter Thirteen

Cadillac Dave jumped out of his sound sleep when the hotel phone rang to inform him that it was checkout time. His head was pounding due his drinking the night before. He remembered calling up Twin and her coming over but nothing else.

"Yo, ma, you wanna go get some breakfast?" Cadillac Dave thought Twin was in the bathroom, but when he didn't get a response, he got up out of the bed to find that she was gone and so were his things.

"Damn, that fucking bitch!" He yelled out, standing in just his boxers. He became even more vexed when he discovered that his clothes were gone too. He needed to call his boy, Black, so that he could bring him some fresh gear to put on. He tried calling Twin's cell phone, but there was no answer.

"Please, somebody answer," his heart pounded, impatiently awaiting an answer.

"Yo, what up?" answered Black.

"Yo, I need you to bring me a pair of jeans and a shirt." Cadillac Dave looked around the room to see if his sneakers were gone too. "Oh, and some kicks to, man."

"Yo, nigga, what happened? Where you at?" Black questioned.

"Man, I'm at the Doubletree next to the airport. Yo, that fucking bitch done robbed me for my shit and bounced on a nigga while I was sleeping. Thank God I valet parked, 'cause the bitch probably would've taken my car keys too."

"Who?" asked Black, while laughing.

"Bitch name Twin." Cadillac Dave said real sour.

"Yo, man, for real. That's one of my ol' lady friends. Man, I done told you about picking up stray bitches."

"Man, fuck all that. Just bring me some clothes. I'm in room 462, come see me." He hung up and immediately dialed Twin's cell phone. The bitch still didn't answer.

Von Diesel

## Chapter Fourteen

Princess was experiencing a burning and itching sensation in her pussy. It was the worst kind of discomfort that she had ever felt in her life. "I swear if Marcus done gave me something, I'll kill his ass," she thought.

Even though she had started making him wear condoms ever since he admitted to sleeping around on her, all types of disgusting thoughts crossed her mind.

"What if he gave me something that I can't get rid of, like herpes or maybe even AIDS?"

Princess loved Marcus and through all of his wrongdoings, she was still trying to hold on, but if he had given her a sexually transmitted disease, she would never be able to forgive him. Sure, he fucked around, but she dealt with it as long as he respected her enough to at least use protection.

She kept her discomfort from Marcus and held out from sex for a couple of days hoping it would go away, but it didn't.

She didn't know which was worse, fighting off Marcus, or trying to soothe the irritation with every coochie cream CVS and Rite-Aid carried.

Finally, she couldn't take it anymore. So, she went to the clinic to find out what was wrong. Going to the department of health was embarrassing, especially because it was located on Fulton Industrial and everybody hung out on the boulevard, so the chances of not being seen were slim.

Princess paced back and forth in front of the building for about ten minutes before she went inside, but that was the easy part. The hard part was not running into a familiar face while inside the waiting room, because more than likely if you were there, it was to treat an STD of some kind.

She quickly scanned the room as she walked over to the front desk to get a number and fill out a questionnaire. She was relieved when she didn't recognize any of the faces.

The wait was about an hour before her number was called. Inside the office the doctor handed her a few brochures and asked her all types of questions regarding her sexual history before asking her the nature of her visit. After explaining her discomfort, Princess was asked if she'd like to be tested for HIV.

"No, I just want to know what's causing my irritation," she quickly responded. Princess would not want to live if she found out she had AIDS, so she declined being tested for the virus.

The doctor didn't agree with her decision, but she didn't push the issue. She told Princess to get undressed and lie back on the table.

Princess was so uncomfortable. The doctor told her to relax and talked her through the examination. In minutes, it was over, and Princess was told to get dressed and return to the waiting room until the nurse called her for blood and urine samples.

As she walked down the hallway, reading the information the doctor had given her, someone called out her name.

"Princess!"

Princess heart dropped when she heard the familiar voice. She looked up and spotted Rhapsodee, dressed in one of those two-piece blue hospital uniforms.

Fuck, Princess thought. Out of all people, why did she have to run into her?

"Girl, what are you doing here?" Rhapsodee asked as she approached her.

Princess rolled her eyes. That's the last question she wanted to be asked right now.

Before Princess could respond, her number was called. "Oh, hey, that's me, I gotta go. I'll call you later, love you."

The nurse took her blood test first, then handed her a cup and asked her to go to the bathroom and bring back some urine. Once she brought the urine sample back, the nurse gave her a pregnancy test, and in minutes, A negative result came back. Unfortunately, her discharge sample came back positive for Chlamydia. The nurse told her that it was a sexually transmitted disease, but the good news was it was curable. She gave Princess an antibiotic injection and informed her that it would take up to five days for her blood work to come back from the lab confirming whether she had any other STDs.

It took a lot to break through her thick skin, but she had just reached her limit with the bullshit. With tears streaming down her face, she wasn't going to take it no more. She lost herself a long time ago, fucking with Marcus, but loving him was no longer worth her dignity. She put up with his ass whippings, his verbal abuse, and even his cheating. Marcus owed her more than this, because she had always been there for him. Being that down-ass bitch wasn't cute no more.

# Von Diesel

## Chapter Fifteen

Leah heard a knock at the door. "Who the fuck is this at my door at two uh...muthafuckin' clock in the morning?"

"Yo, Leah, It's D'Lamar. Open up," he yelled.

"I'm coming. Stop knocking on my fucking door like you crazy," Leah yelled back as she cracked open the door.

"Yo, what up, Leah?" asked D'Lamar in a playful tone.

"E-Love ain't here," Leah snobbishly responded.

"I ain't here for him!"

"Then what chu' want?"

"Yo, Leah, what's up? Cause I'm saying, you been throwing me a lot of shade lately, especially when ya boy, E-Love be around."

"Ain't nothing up." Leah stepped back to let D'Lamar come inside.

"Oh, so I'm bugging out then, right?"

"Look, D'Lamar, I don't know what you talking about."

"I'm saying, Leah, every time I come through, you start rolling your eyes, huffing and puffing and shit. Like a nigga did something to you. All I wanna know is, what the fuck is up with all that?" D'Lamar carried on.

"Whatever, D'Lamar. Look, It's late and I'm tired, so uh---"

"Nah, ain't no 'so uhhhh'. So, let me finish."

"What do you want D'Lamar?" Leah rolled her eyes, and let out a hard sigh, making sure he knew how annoyed she was getting.

"Yo, how's what's her face doing?" Skirting around for the real reason for his visit.

Leah was getting defensive and stared D'Lamar down. She ignored his question for a few moments, assuming he was asking about Lucky to be sarcastic.

"Yo, I don't know who you're talking about, and honestly, I don't give a fuck, so why are you wasting my time?"

"Lucky, that's her name," said D'Lamar.

"What is it to you?" she questioned.

"Nothing really, but since she's your friend, I just thought I'd ask. Either way, that's neither here nor there, cause that ain't why I'm here," said D'Lamar.

"Then what is the reason?"

"Business, of course," D'Lamar replied.

"What business you got to discuss with me?" Leah asked with a puzzled look on her face.

"Your little business down at the Candy Shop."

"What about it?" asked Leah.

"I heard you were doing well for yourself down there, before you started selling real estate."

"Oh yeah, that's what you heard?"

"Yeah, that's exactly what I heard. Instead of lap dancing for that bull-shit ass money you were making, you were charging thirty dollars a pop for E. I'm really impressed."

"So, what you saying, D'Lamar?"

"I'm saying, I'm trying to be on your team."

"What team? I'm done with that life."

"Oh really? Cause I fucked this stripper bitch a little while ago at the Candy Shop who said you be making fifteen G's a week. Now that's a nice little piece of change. So since I know your man hates dykes and you're into girls, you should be looking out for a brother. Say forty percent and I'll keep your secret."

"Forty percent, of what? You're bugging the fuck out if you think I'm giving you my money," Leah yelled.

"A'ight then, I guess I'ma have to tell E-Love, and you know how that nigga feel about that shit."

"Yo, I can't believe you D'Lamar. If it wasn't for me, you wouldn't be making the money you making now. I helped you out, and now you trying to play me. It's all good, though, nigga. You do dirt, you gon' get dirt."

"Oh, I'm so scared."

"You'll get your forty percent. Just go, get the fuck out of my house!"

D'Lamar slowly walked out the door past Leah, who was holding it open. She slammed it right behind him. He was kind of surprised at how easy it was to get Leah to agree to his terms.

"You muthafucka!" she stormed into the bedroom and grabbed her cell phone. Her heart raced with anger as she dialed Seven's number.

"What's up with you putting my fucking business out there like that, and to a nigga you don't even know?"

"Yo, Leah, hold up. Pump your breaks for a minute 'cause I don't know what you talking about," said Seven.

"Oh, you don't know what I'm talking about, huh?"

"Nah, and you shouldn't even coming at me with this bullshit," Seven replied.

"So, you ain't fuck this nigga named D'Lamar?" Leah asked.

"Yeah, I fucked him, but I ain't tell him shit, that's my word. This is what happened. The nigga got a lap dance from me a couple of nights ago, right? Then he starts asking me questions, like do I sell E, and who I work for. So, I got a little paranoid, and I back off from the nigga, then I start asking some of the girls some questions about him. They told me he hustled, and shit was gravy with the nigga, so I'm like, cool."

"Now, I'm more relaxed around the nigga, last time I saw him was tonight. The vibe was good, so I went to the hotel with him, but I swear I ain't mention your name. That's my word on everything I love, on my son at that. Did that nigga tell you some bogus shit?"

"Yep, but it's all good." Leah was pissed.

"Yo, that's my word, Leah. I wouldn't do no shiesty shit like that to you, and if you got that nigga's number, we can straighten this shit out now!"

"How you fuck a nigga and don't get his number?" Leah wondered.

"Nah, don't even worry about it. I'll check you tomorrow."

"A'ight, see you then." Seven said.

"One more thing, Seven...you didn't say anything about what went on with me and Lucky did you?"

"No, never!"

Now Leah was furious, and at this point she didn't know what or who to believe. She knew somebody was ratting her out.

As she hung up the phone, it rang again. She didn't even get the chance to say hello, before D'Lamar yelled in the phone..."Oh yeah, I forgot to tell you that E-Love was in jail. He got busted coming out of Miami with five kilos of coke." Before she could say anything, he hung up.

She immediately called her mother-in-law and gave her the bad news. Her mother-in-law told her to bring the twins over to her house for Meek to babysit, while she and Leah took a little trip to Miami to find out what's going on with her son.

Leah got dressed, rounded up the twins and their bags and headed out the door.

## Chapter Sixteen

Black and Sosa made their way to the Doubletree. They parked and then made their way to the elevator. Once off, they walked the hallway until they spotted room 462.

Black knocked three times waiting for Cadillac Dave to answer.

"Yo, what up my nigga?" asked Black.

"Man, shit crazy. I can't believe ol' girl took my clothes and shit and ran off with them," Cadillac Dave complained.

"What up Sosa, long time no see," said Cadillac Dave while giving him a pound.

"Ain't nuthin', man," Sosa answered.

"So, what y'all got going on?" asked Cadillac Dave.

"We 'bout to ride on down to New Orleans to see Papa Doc about doing a lil' business. They say he doing it big my nigga. Shid…I gotta eat and the streets in Atlanta is dry as fuck. Ain't shit going on," Black complained.

"Ain't Papa Doc and Big Earl running partnas?" asked Cadillac Dave.

"Yeah, him and pops been making moves since the early 80s. That nigga got old money, know what I mean?" spat Black.

"So, do Big Earl know you going down there to see him?" asked Cadillac Dave.

"Man, fuck all that. Like I said, a nigga gotta eat. I'ma check on his prices and see what he working wit', and if I like what he got, I'ma make some boss moves wit' him." said Black.

"A'ight man, be careful, ya heard me."

"Talk about niggas being careful, look like you need to be sleeping with both eyes opened. Bitch put yo ass to sleep wit' her pussy, then ran off wit' yo shit." Sosa laughed.

"So, who is she, man?" asked Black.

"A chick I met last night at the Sugar Shak, named Twin. I got a room last night 'cause I was too drunk to drive to the crib. I called the bitch up and she came through. I don't even remember if we fucked. But I woke up this morning and she was ghost, and so was my shit."

"Twin?" Black yelled. She about 5'9, 145 pounds, long ass hair, pretty lil' muthafucka'?" asked Black.

"Yeah, you know her or something?"

"Hell yeah, man she my ol' lady friend. And that bitch is straight certified. Aye, yo…how that shit happen?"

"Man, y'all give my shit and get the fuck outta' here."

Black and Sosa laughed all the way out the door.

## Chapter Seventeen

Twin finally answered her cell phone.

"Hello," she answered.

"Yo, how I get to you?" Cadillac Dave asked.

"Well, hello to you, too," Twin said as she glanced over at the clock, which read 2 p.m.

"Oh, my bad. Hello, beautiful. Now how do I get to you once I hit Wesley Chapel?"

Twin smiled, liking his persistence, and gave him directions.

"A'ight, I should be there in like forty-five minutes. You still got my shit, right?"

"Yes. I hope you didn't think the worst of me, I figured if I took your stuff, you'd have no choice but to come back and see me."

"Woman, you wild. Bring a few things, just in case I decide to kidnap you for a couple of days."

"Okay, I'll see you when you get here." After ending the call, Twin excitedly jumped out of bed to search through her many clothes for the right outfits to pack. She decided to wear her hot ping Roberto Cavalli sundress, along with her Prada sandals and matching purse. She packed three other cute outfits that showed expensive taste, class, and style. By no means did she want him to think she was anything less than fabulous.

Cadillac Dave pulled in front of Twin's crib and phoned her to come outside. When she reached the front door, she fell in love with his sparkling Silver Hummer. Not the affordable Hummer H2. This was the real deal.

"What's up, sexy? Don't I get a kiss?" asked Cadillac Dave as he held the car door open for her.

"Nah, I don't kiss on the first date," Twin laughed.

"I respect that. So last night wasn't our first date?" asked Cadillac Dave.

"No, it was our first night of conversation," explained Twin.

"Yo, you funny girl," said Cadillac Dave.

"Whatever," Twin replied.

"Last night I was so drunk, I had to get a room. I don't believe in drinking and driving."

"Oh, yeah," she said as she sniffed the air...."Maybe not drinking and driving, but definitely smoking and flying." The both of them laughed in unison.

Twin gave him back his clothes, shoes and jewelry.

"Preciate it, ma," spat Cadillac Dave.

"No problem," said Twin. In her mind she was thinking that she was gonna fuck the shit out of that nigga.

Cadillac Dave picked up the phone and told his cook to start preparing breakfast for two.

"You like omelets?" he asked.

"Yeah, they're all right," Twin answered.

"Well, my chef, Karter, makes some banging ass omelets. You'll love 'em."

Twenty minutes later, they pulled up to a tall black gate that Cadillac Dave opened with a little remote. Twin was still trying to get over the fact that he had a chef when he pulled into a four-car garage next to a convertible black Bentley.

"This is so beautiful, she thought as she looked around the grounds. He got out of the driver's side and rushed to open the door for her again. He was the perfect gentleman. His $2.5 million, six-bedroom house was located in ultra-chic Atlanta and came equipped with an in-ground swimming pool, sauna, huge patio, and a basketball court. Indoors was a gym, a small movie theater and a game room.

Twin had to admit that this was far more impressive than any nice car or house she'd ever seen in her life. This was the type of lifestyle that she was born to live. She was tired of dealing with the small-time hustlers in the hood, who were satisfied with the minimum--a little bit of jewelry, a hot ride, fifty grand stashed in an old sneaker box, and a laced-out apartment in the projects, thinking life is sweet. She wanted to live like a celebrity. If she played her cards right, Cadillac Dave could be her ticket straight outta' the ghetto.

He escorted her straight to the kitchen for the best breakfast she ever had. After breakfast, Cadillac Dave gave Twin a personal tour.

This house is definitely made for MTV cribs, she thought as they entered the master bedroom. It had a brick fireplace, a king size bed with plush feather pillows, and a matching cream-colored comforter. The bathroom was all marble, with an oval-shaped Jacuzzi and an attached shower. His walk-in closet was bigger than the bedroom in Twin's apartment, and being the fashion fanatic that she was, she couldn't help but take a look inside. According to her, you could tell a lot about a person from his or her style of dress.

Once side of his closet had at least two hundred pairs of jeans and button-up shirts from every designer neatly hanging up, stacks of starter hats on the shelves, velour sweat suits, about fifty pairs of white-on-white air force ones, five pairs of Jordan's, a couple of Sean Carters, and too many pairs of Timbs to count. Twin could tell by judging the number of suits and shoes he owned, that he wasn't big on dressing up, but when he did, at least he did his thing by rocking designer names like Ralph Loren, Gucci, and Armani. Last but not least, she glided her hands up and down his mink jackets and butter soft leathers.

She couldn't help but hum the tune *Why Don't We Fall in Love* by Amerie. Why not? He had everything she wanted and more.

# Von Diesel

## Chapter Eighteen

Rhapsodee made it the gift shop, then made her way to Swerve's room carrying "Get well soon" balloons and some flowers. She had only half an hour left before morning visiting hours were over. Seeing Swerve was something she had to do, but her mind couldn't stop wondering about Black. He'd been ignoring her calls.

*Is he with someone else*, she thought? Regardless of the circumstances, she felt she was still his fiancé, and there was no excuse for his behavior.

As Rhapsodee entered the room she felt sick. She hated to see Swerve hooked up to all of those tubes.

Rhapsodee walked closer to Swerve's bedside. Seeing Swerve lying there like that brought Rhapsodee to tears. She pulled up a chair and moved in as close as she could to the side of the bed. Taking Swerve's hand into hers, she began to talk to him.

"Hi baby, it's me, Rhapsodee. I know you're in bad shape right now, but you're gonna pull through this. I know you will, because you know the world can't make it without you, James St. John." She let out a little laugh. "We just can't do it without you, baby, so you better hurry up and get better before I go crazy. You're my husband and I still love you."

"I gotta go now, but I'll be back tomorrow," Rhapsodee said, as she kissed Swerve on his forehead and headed out the door.

# Von Diesel

## Chapter Nineteen

I opened my eyes and looked at the bricks and bars surrounding me. I can't believe this shit.

I was hoping this whole shit was a nightmare, but come to find out, I wasn't dreaming at all. My dick ached, my stomach was growling, and I needed a fucking spliff. I hopped off my bunk and headed to the phone. I hit up one of my jump-off bitches from Tampa.

She accepted the collect call right away. "What's up baby?"

"Fucked up shortie. Thanks for taking the call. You know I got you."

"You know I got your back, boo."

"Look, I need you to make a call for me on three-way."

"Not a problem."

I then called out D'Lamar's number.

D'Lamar answered right away, "Yo, what's up?"

"Man, it's a long story. I'll fill you in on that shit later. Right now, I need you to call my people back home and let them know what's up, so they can get shit lined up to get me out this bitch. Then, I need you to handle things with your boy in Sandy Springs for me. You gon' have to hold down the fort until I get this shit straight. You feel me?"

"Nuff said, nigga. Say no more. You know I got you. I'ma jump on shit right now. Gone." D'Lamar hung up the phone.

A few minutes later, the recording came on, warning us we had one minute left on the phone, so we wrapped things up and ended the call.

I returned to my bunk and tried to map something out. I knew I needed to get in touch with Leah and my mom's. They were the only ones I could really depend on to handle my money and make sure the lawyer was paid.

I'd learned my lesson about letting jump-off bitches hold money. That situation I had in the past when I was fucking with Twin had taught me well. I had got locked up and had her collect my money, when it came time for her to pay my lawyer, no money was to be found. I had to straight shoot that bitch just to get my shit back.

But to be honest, this time it was that nigga D'Lamar, I was a little worried about. I swear, lately that nigga had been on some bullshit. I couldn't quite put my finger on it, but it was just something about him that I just wasn't feeling.

After a few days had passed. I went for my first bond hearing and it was denied. I kinda expected that shit though. These muthafucka's wasn't trying to let a nigga out. Hell, I was a major flight risk. There was no way these niggas were gonna take a chance with me.

Even with all those odds against me, Felecia, my lawyer was still talking some good shit. She was confident that I would eventually get a bond and was telling me it may take a couple of tries. One thing about her though, her word was bond. She didn't sell a nigga a dream. She was always on her shit, and never let a nigga down.

It was visiting day, and cats were getting fresh cuts and edge-ups and shit, trying to look fly for their chics. I wasn't fucking with none of that shit though. For one, I couldn't see myself sitting between another nigga's legs while he braided my fucking hair. Next thing I know, I ain't getting no fucking visit.

I hopped in my bunk, grabbed my dick and rubbed on it until I fell asleep.

"Langford!" The CO called out my last name, waking me.

"Yo!" I yelled back.

"Visit."

"Damn! Who the fuck is that?" I wondered who the hell had come down to check on a nigga. I hadn't even bothered telling no one my visiting day.

I followed the CO to the visiting room. I was surprised to see my wife and moms when I walked out. I wondered what the fuck they were doing here and how the hell they knew my visiting day. A nigga was actually glad to see a familiar face. I was grinning from ear to ear as I sat on the steel stool across from then.

"What y'all doing here?"

"What you mean? There is no way I was gonna leave my baby alone in jail."

"Ma, y'all ain't have to come down here."

"Well, we wanted to make sure everything was okay," his mother chimed in. "We going to see Felecia and straighten her out tomorrow."

"Yeah, go 'head and pay her. That's the most important thing. Everything else can wait. You talked to D'Lamar, Leah?"

"Yep. That's one reason I wanted to come here. I don't know what's up with your boy. Baby, I know you ain't gonna wanna hear this, but that nigga made a pass at me."

"What the fuck you say? Leah, don't fuck with me."

"He came to the house in the wee hours of the fucking morning. He kept making little comments about how my ass was so phat and what he'll do to me, and some shit about you ain't gon' be around to satisfy me, so I may as well give it up to him. He was talking so crazy, I had to ask this nigga if he was drunk or on that shit. The next thing I know, he grabs my ass. I was sure he'd lost his fucking mind. I had to smack some sense back into his ass. After that, I cussed his ass out and made him leave. I haven't heard from him since. I even called him a few times and left messages about the paper, but he ain't called back. He acts like he is dodging niggas or something. Then I hear the streets saying D'Lamar talking like you ain't never getting out, and he's the new boss. This nigga can't be trusted baby. He was the one who told me you got popped with five keys."

"What?" It was like I could literally feel my blood boiling inside as I listened to what Leah was saying. How did D'Lamar know about the five keys? He had to be in on this shit with them crooked as blues. It felt as though my back was against the wall. I was ready to kill a nigga, but I knew beating another nigga's ass in jail to blow off steam wasn't going to do nothing but add more charges to my rap sheet. One of the worst things in the world was knowing a bitch-ass nigga was tripping on the streets and it ain't shit you can do about it. Bobby B was right about that nigga.

After my visit with my moms and wifey, I wondered how the fuck I was going to make it through.

Five days had passed, which felt more like months, and the two special ladies in my life had already paid my lawyer in full. As usual, she was on her grind. I knew the time would soon arrive when I would be released from Dade County Jail. And I knew when I was released, I'd be on an unstoppable mission to get my fucking money. The first stop after getting me some pussy would be a visit to check D'Lamar. I wondered if he was going to like having a gun in his damn mouth, or a knife clinging to his throat.

## Chapter Twenty

After talking to E-Love, I was fucking vexed. I had stood by that nigga's side for years, never deceiving him, stealing from him, or trying to shave off his profit. There was no other nigga that had his back like me, and this was the thanks I get? Not wanting to sit and dwell on him and his bullshit, I decided to go to the pool hall and kick it with some of my niggas and have a few beers.

"Damn nigga! Fuck wrong wit' you coming up in here like you wanna kill niggas and shit," said Lucky, one of the pool sharks as soon as I walked in the place. Lucky was a dominant ole' dyke ass female who was caking all the ladies. I eyed her baggy fittin' True Religion jeans and Ed Hardy skull t-shirt. She was dressed like a straight dude. Once out of earshot to the public, I began to fill her in.

"Nah, it ain't no beef shit. I just got off the phone with that nigga E-Love, and that nigga be talking to me like I'm some little bitch. He needs to start respecting me. You feel me?"

"Right, right." Lucky didn't say much. Her, like most niggas, was too afraid to curse E-Love.

The more I thought about things it really started to get under my skin. I had to wonder what the fuck this nigga took me for. After everything I'd done for homie, all the fucking wars we'd been through and I had this nigga back, this nigga was still talking to me like I was some little nothing-ass nigga. I'd been past the toy soldier status. A nigga had his wings now, but E-Love couldn't see it. But whether he chose to see it or not, I knew I wasn't gonna be his "Gofer" for too much longer. It was definitely time for a change.

Although I'd never crossed E-Love before, I was really considering it. I was making just enough money to get by working with him. It was time for me to make a come up. I figured the next time that nigga gave me some shit to deliver, or some money to collect, I was gonna take that shit and flip it and make a little money off of it, then pay him. As long as I did that shit quickly, he would never know the difference. After a few flips, I would have enough money on my own to start buying some weight.

Von Diesel

## Chapter Twenty-One

Twin was enjoying her time with Cadillac Dave so much she didn't want it to end. In twenty-four hours, they had already managed to do so much. He had bought her a Gucci Bikini to swim in, amongst other things. They spent half the night talking. Her stay felt more like a mini vacation away from the hood, and it made her realize just how much she was ready for some changes in her life. Being with Cadillac Dave was a different experience for her. He had the means to expose her to a whole new world, not to mention the other qualities she required: money, money and more money.

Cadillac Dave grew up on the rough streets of D.C., doing the norm--stealing cars, robbing niggas, and hustling. Even though he was fortunate to make it out of the hood, Twin admired the fact that he was still street unlike some niggas who were quick to switch to that Hollywood shit. He also had other characteristics, sense of humor, and of course, his big feet and hands, assuming the myth was true.

Cadillac Dave was feeling Twin's personality, which she worked to the fullest. He felt comfortable around her. She didn't appear to be fake, like most of the bitches he ran across. Plus, she could relate to his struggles, and to top it off, he found her absolutely gorgeous.

Sitting on the patio, smoking weed, Cadillac Dave entertained Twin with crazy stories about his past. To him her beauty was such a natural one that it made a nigga weak at the knees.

Twin was having a lot of fun with him, but all this fun was making her horny. She wanted him badly and felt as though she would die from lack of dick if he didn't make a move soon.

She wasn't used to being around a guy for more than ten minutes that didn't try to fuck her. Cadillac Dave was in the dope game, so Twin assumed he wouldn't be pressed for pussy, since all types of chicks probably came at him. One thing was certain from his hard on in the bed last night. He was definitely attracted to her, still and all, Twin wanted to maintain a respectable "Take home to mama type of image," so she fell back on initiating sex of any kind.

Cadillac Dave sat in his plush leather chair, staring at Twin. Then out of nowhere, he pulled her closer to him and started to fondle her body as though he had read her mind. Twin straddled her legs across his lap and stuck her tongue in his mouth, for their first real kiss.

Damn, he can kiss, she thought as his tongue motion flowed with hers perfectly.

Cadillac Dave started to undress her. He went to unbutton her shirt but noticed some resistance every time he made an attempt to remove it.

She didn't want him to go there, but she didn't say anything. Instead, she just redirected his focus by getting down on her knees and releasing his manhood.

Thank God the myth does apply. She opened her mouth and took in as much of his thickness as she possibly could. He was so big that she could only fit half of his dick in her mouth. Just like any pro, Twin was up for the challenge. She was determined to taste every inch of him, licking down the sides of his stiffness as he moaned and she lubricated his dick with her saliva, stroking her small hands up and down the base.

Cadillac Dave couldn't take it any longer. He wanted to feel inside her walls. "Ahh, man wait! I want some pussy 'cause I know it's good." Lifting himself up just enough to pull a condom from his back pocket, he passed it to her and smiled.

Twin stood up and unfastened her Seven jeans. Stepping out of them, she slowly rolled the magnum down on his horse-sized dick and was ready to ride.

"Wait. Let me see you play with yourself." Cadillac Dave prolonged insertion as his way of teasing her. Twin smiled. She knew the game and played it well as she leaned back on the recliner and started to lick on her fingers until they were shiny from her saliva. Then, cocking her legs up, she slid two of her fingers inside herself and began to move them in and out of her pussy.

"Ummmmm," she moaned as her pussy became drenched with juice. Withdrawing her fingers from inside of her, she inserted them in his mouth.    Cadillac Dave sucked on them like they were popsicles and then dove in headfirst between her legs for more.

"Ooooh, I wanna cum." Twin breathed heavily.

"Don't cum yet. I want you to sit on my dick and cum."

Without holding back, Twin mounted his manhood and slowly stroked him, not quite ready to endure the pain it would've caused if she slammed down on it right away.    Once her pussy walls adjusted to his fullness.    It was on and popping.    She worked it, popping her pussy, bouncing up and down on his dick like a wild woman, until they both exploded.

Von Diesel

## Chapter Twenty-Two

When I'd gotten home from the barbershop, I'd planned to let Rhapsodee's ass have it. But the rational side of me just couldn't allow that to happen so quickly. It took all I had, but I went on with the day as usual while I decided on the best way to approach things.

I was the type of nigga that liked to have all my ducks in a row, so when I came with it, I came hard. I liked to be confident that it wasn't shit a bitch or nigga could say to lie there way out of things. I knew I was about to make a hell of an allegation, so I wanted to be sure I had my facts straight when I did it.

After running that day at the barbershop through my head over and over, along with all the other shit that had happened, I was sure that bitch was on some shiesty shit. My fucking blood was boiling as I waited patiently for her to walk through the door.

When she got home, she rushed up to me all kissy poo and shit. She was wearing a pair of pink Bebe shorts hiked all the way up her ass and a white Bebe tank, showing every curve of her body. I had to admit, the shit was tempting, but that wasn't going to work this day. I had to give it to her though. She was a good actress, just like her hoe ass friend Twin. She could've won a fucking academy award for the act she put on, and she could have really fooled an amateur, but I wasn't buying the bullshit she was selling.

"Baby come check out my bridesmaid's colors. They're going to wear lavender. I don't want no ghetto-looking colors. Yeah baby, this wedding is gonna have class all the way."

I followed Rhapsodee to her computer room, where she had the latest bridal magazines spread out on the floor, an indication that she had gone too far.

The last count I had, this broad had spent about fifty thousand on the wedding, and we ain't even walked down the aisle. Just thinking about it made steam come out of my ears.

"Baby, what's the matter?" she asked, her face twisted into a corkscrew of concern.

This made me all the madder, that she could sound so innocent. "Yeah, right, Bitch! You know what's the matter." I grabbed her by the neck and looked her in the eye.

She looked all surprised and shit. "No, I don't, baby. What is it? I ain't no mind reader!"

"I can't believe you'd do me like this!"

"What are you talking about?" asked Rhapsodee.

"I know you been out at Grady visiting that nigga. So you playing wifey to that nigga or something?" spat Black.

"What? I'm with you every day. I sleep with you every night. How do I have the time to play wifey with Swerve?"

"Well, you gone tell me something, before I get pissed the fuck off. I should have never fucked with you in the first place. What the fuck I look like to you? Boo-boo the fool? You must take me for some little bitch. You really got me fucked up Rhapsodee. Do your thing, ma. Be wit' that nigga. I'm out!"

Black grabbed his keys, and walked out the front door, never looking back. He was fuming as he drove. He didn't know where he was headed, but he knew he needed to get the fuck away from Rhapsodee.

Finally cooling off a little bit, he pulled up to Dudley's Bar and Grill. As soon as he walked in, he felt right at home. The atmosphere hadn't changed a bit.

He hadn't been sitting a whole minute before he felt someone staring a whole through the center of his back. He turned around to see this fine ass bitch wit' hella hips and ass walking his way.

"Hi, handsome. My name's Yoshi. You wanna buy me a drink?"

## Chapter Twenty-Three

"What up, D'Lamar?" Lucky gave me a pound as I walked in the pool hall.

"Ain't shit, nigga. Look like money, smell like money, you know the song, nigga," I said, feeling on top of the world.

Now that E-Love was locked up, I was the king of the castle. I'd used the product I'd gotten from Detective Stixx and Raybon-Brown and flipped it a few times. Finally, a nigga was making his own money and not taking orders. This was the opportunity I'd been waiting for. From the looks of things, E-Love was never gonna see daylight, so I was on some real "fuck-you" shit. I had his shit, I was doing what the fuck I wanted to, and I wasn't afraid to let niggas know it. I had a new attitude. It was time for niggas on the street to know D'Lamar wasn't E-Love's little bitch.

I walked through the pool hall straight to the back, where some dudes were playing a dice game. Feeling a little lucky with my new profile, I got in on the game.

Flame, one of the guys in the dice game, held them in front of a chick who was watching the action. "Blow on these dice for me baby." She blew on the dice. Then he rolled them. "Bam! Pay up nigga, pay up!" Flame hit, and I lost one hundred dollars just like that.

"Damn, baby girl! You must be good luck. Let me rub these dice on that ass this time. Nah, matter of fact, let me rub them on your ass, pussy and tits."

"Man, shut the fuck up and roll the fucking dice!" I yelled, getting pissed off by the bullshit this nigga was doing.

"Man, fuck you, D'Lamar!" He snapped back.

Flame wasn't no big nigga on the streets, but he was known for bullying a nigga and taking their shit.

"Fuck you say nigga?" I stood up. If Flame had the chance to tackle me, it would be Game over.

Flame stood up now, towering over me. "Nigga you heard me!"

"Nigga, you better recognize what the fuck is good and step the fuck back. I run these fucking streets, nigga." I had to man up. If

I gave the slightest indication of weakness, this bully would have definitely tried to overpower me.

"Whatever, dude. You come in this bitch talking shit like you on top of the fucking world when just the other week you were in here crying like a fucking baby, talking about how E-Love don't respect your bitch ass. I overheard the conversation between you and Lucky. Nigga, shut the fuck up!" Flame took two fingers and mushed D'Lamar in his forehead.

When Flame stood up and mushed him in his head, he had taken shit too far. He knew it was either do or die at that point. So, with his reputation on the line, D'Lamar knew he couldn't back down. He pulled out his gun and gave Flame one big forceful strike across his face.

*BAM!*

One hit and the dude fell to the ground.

"Now who's the bitch?" D'Lamar said to him as blood flowed from his lip.

"DAAAAMMMMNNNN! You just got knocked the fuck out!" Another guy jokingly quoted the words from the movie *Friday* when Deebo got knocked out.

As everyone else busted out in laughter at his antics, Flame walked away.

The constant joking must have been too much for him to handle because, just as D'Lamar got to the door of the pool hall, he heard a lot of commotion behind him. Before he could turn around, he heard shots.

*POP! POP! POP!*

D'Lamar dove between two cars and pulled his gun out. He looked up to see dude rushing to a car. He shot back at him.

*BAM! BAM!*

D'Lamar watched as Flame fell to the ground. He wasn't sure where he was hit, but at least he was down. D'Lamar jumped in his whip and peeled off, never looking back.

## Chapter Twenty-Four

It was day two since they hit skins, and still no Black in sight, not even a courtesy call. Rhapsodee tried reaching him on his cell, but after leaving several messages, she gave up. There was only one word to describe how she felt; played.

If this is Black's way of making her feel like shit on the bottom of his shoe, well, damn it, he's done it.

Tears began to run down her face, and the feeling of loneliness came over her.

Maybe he's seeing someone else, she thought. All the signs are right in my face. He won't answer my calls. He can't be living out of a hotel all this time. Where the fuck is he? I guess out with his new girl.

"That has to be it!" she cried out. Her assumptions made everything seem all too clear.

She got out of bed and started packing all of Black's belongings.

"If you want to be with somebody else, that's fine, but you won't do it here," she screamed out while throwing all his things into garbage bags. "I'm done with the apologies and making an ass out of myself over and over."

Rhapsodee struggled as she dragged the bags down the steps and left them by the front door. Then she dialed Leah, who, of course, didn't answer.

"Black, this is Rhapsodee, and since you haven't bothered to return any of my calls, don't. Just come and get your stuff. It's already packed and waiting by the door, so the hard part is over. Good-bye." Rhapsodee exhaled as she plopped down to the floor and new tears began to fall, replacing the dry ones.

She took a moment to collect her thoughts, but all she kept asking herself was, damn, how could I be so stupid? He's not coming back.

Still holding the phone in her hand, she decided to try Leah again, but she didn't want her to know she was entering a second failed relationship. She laid back down as tears began to wet her pillow.

# Von Diesel

## Chapter Twenty-Five

Weeks had passed, and still no one had heard from D'Lamar's little bitch ass. I'd heard he'd gotten into a little beef on the streets and ended up killing the neighborhood bully, Flame. That shit was a surprise to me. I guess he was really out there feeling himself, trying to act like he was the big man in town. The stories I was hearing about him really had me going. I couldn't believe this nigga really thought he was the boss. I was convinced he had bucked on me for my money and that was how he had his little come up. I'd spent each day thinking about how the fuck I was gonna deal with him and was just hoping Flame's boys didn't get him first.

Bucking on my money was bucking on the Haitians' money. And I didn't have the army to go to war with those niggas. Hell, I was already skating on thin ice, because I was down on my supply.

My first instinct was to just get out of jail, hunt his bitch ass down, and straight kill him, but then I started to think on a whole different level. After pulling a few strings, I was able to get one of his hoes to give him a call on three-way. I finally had the opportunity to holla at that nigga.

Of course, I had to ask him about that shit with Leah first. That was a true violation. There is no way a nigga could feel up my wife and get away with it. Then I asked about my money, and about the shit niggas was saying on the streets. And, like the bitch I knew he was, D'Lamar denied it all. He gave me some lame excuse about getting robbed, when it came to the money, he had managed to collect on half before he got robbed though. I made that nigga think everything was all good and there was no beef. Plus, when that nigga found out I had another bond hearing coming up and I was definitely getting out on that one, he straightened his act up. At first, he thought I would never see daylight, so he was trying to flex, but when the reality hit that I was coming home, that nigga switched the whole thing up.

Just like wifey had promised, me and Bobby B went before the judge and got a bond. We gathered up our shit, preparing to be released. A nigga never felt so happy. Two months in jail was way too much time for a cat like me. It took three different judges and three different bond hearings for us to get a bond. The judge set it at one million dollars each, with hopes that we would never get out, but it only took one phone call and one hundred grand each, and we were on the road the same fucking day.

Now that we were hitting the streets, it was straight to business. I had to get my wife piped up with this good ole' wood, and D'Lamar had to be dealt with.

When they released us, we walked out to the gate and there was wifey, parked outside.

## Chapter Twenty-Six

Twin woke up and instantly went into a funk after overhearing Cadillac Dave booking a flight for New York leaving that night. Her little vacation with him was over before she was ready for it to be. She wondered if he would ever call her again and hoped that her time spent with him wasn't a complete waste, because yes, she had a great time, but she wasn't doing it for nothing. Twin wanted to be rescued from the hood by a wealthy knight in platinum armor and live glamorously and happily ever after. That was the ghetto fairy tale she was hoping for.

"Good Morning, beautiful," Cadillac Dave said as he plopped down next to her on the bed. Right off the bat, he sensed a bit of attitude by the way she twisted up her lips and cut her eyes at him. "What's up? You okay?" he asked.

"Yeah, I'm okay." she said.

"You don't seem okay, so tell me what's wrong."

"Nothing. I just overheard you making travel plans, and I guess I wasn't ready for it to be over with us," Twin said.

"Oh, so it's over between us?" Cadillac Dave questioned.

"I don't know, you tell me," she answered.

"Nah, as long as you don't want it to be over, it ain't."

"And what do you want?" Twin asked.

"Well, first, I wanna know why you won't let me kiss on your tits?"

"Cadillac Dave, come on. Be serious!"

"I am serious. I wanna know why every time we have sex, you did everything to deter me from seeing them." He thought that maybe she had gotten a bad boob job or something of that nature.

Twin's eyes started to tear up. He was right. She did stop him from removing her shirt every time they had sex, but it wasn't because of her tits. It was because of the ugly scar she was hiding. She really didn't know how she was gonna explain it. Slowly removing her shirt, she thought of an explanation.

"What happened to you?" he questioned in shock.

Twin revealed the ugly scar from not only the bullet, but the lung surgery after the shooting.

"I was in an abusive relationship, and when I tried to leave him, he tried to kill me," Twin said.

"Damn, ma. I'm sorry to hear that. Where's his punk ass at now?"

"I don't know," Twin said.

"What do you mean, you don't know? Come on. For some sucker shit like that, he should be under the fucking jail."

"I know, but it didn't turn out that way. Believe me, I wish it did, because maybe then the nightmares would stop, and I wouldn't have to worry about him coming back for me one day. But you know, with you I feel safe, I haven't even thought about it." Her tears continued to fall.

Twin had over-dramatized her story to gain his sympathy, and it worked. Cadillac Dave had seen a lot of crazy stuff go down in his hood when it came to a man and his girl.

Twin's story wasn't farfetched. He could understand a nigga not wanting to let her go, because she was absolutely gorgeous, but what she did for him was more mental than physical. He'd fucked plenty of pretty girls with good pussy, but with Twin, he felt a connection that was real, and that made him want to hold on to her.

"Listen, Twin, I'm feeling you like crazy, and if you feel like I feel and it ain't about the money, then maybe something serious could pop off. I'll be in New York for a couple of weeks, but when I get back, I'm trying to see what's good, a'ight?" He leaned down and kissed her ugly scar.

Twin didn't say a word. She just looked in his eyes and hoped her tearful emotions would say it all. In her mind, she was screaming, I got his ass! Just use what you got to get what you want. All she could think about was a life filled with the finer things, like shopping sprees, VIP status, trips around the world, and maybe even a career in acting.

## Chapter Twenty-Seven

*Ring! Ring!*

Not even a whole hour after I'd left the pool hall, I got a call from Lucky.

"What up Lucky?"

"It ain't good, nigga. You know ole' boy ain't make it. The cops were up here and everything nigga. Ain't nobody but niggas are out to get you, dude. Flame boys say, as soon as they see you, it's straight gun play, no talk."

"What you talking bout' Lucky?" I played stupid, not knowing if the cops were around or if this nigga was trying to set me up.

"I'm just letting you know the deal. Watch your back, homeboy." Lucky then hung up.

I really ain't give a fuck if dude lived or not. As long as I was still breathing, that's all that mattered. Fuck him and his weak-ass crew. I'd been ditched out for the last time and wasn't backing down from no nigga, so any cat who wanted it could bring it.

And, as a matter of fact, fuck Lucky too for calling me with that shit. There was no way he was gonna get me to talk about that shit on the phone. Like I told that nigga, I didn't know what the fuck he was talking about. Right at that point, permanent amnesia had set in. I had no recollection of those events. Who's Flame? And what pool hall?

Von Diesel

## Chapter Twenty-Eight

*You have reached the voicemail box of ---.*

I hung up before the recording could finish. Not hearing Black's voice and wondering what the fuck he was doing and where the hell he was at was driving me crazy. It had been an entire day since our argument and I hadn't heard from him. I had called his phone nonstop for a whole hour straight, and all I got was straight voicemail. It had gotten to the point that I was starting to worry. I even called Sosa's phone and it went to voicemail also.

I didn't know what to think. Was he with another bitch? Was he in trouble?

I'd spent the past day sitting in the house, depressed and crying. I hadn't eaten anything or even bothered to wash my ass or brush my teeth. I picked up the phone to call Leah because she'd called me several times earlier in the day and I didn't even bother to answer. I just wasn't in the mood for conversation.

"Hey girl," I said, trying to sound a little upbeat.

"Rhapsodee? Leah asked, not even recognizing her voice.

"Yeah, it's me. I'm down in the dumps, sad as hell."

"Awww, what's wrong boo?" Leah asked, sounding concerned.

I explained to her the drama I had with Black from the beginning to end.

"I'm sorry to hear that. I'm coming over. Get up and get yourself together. We're gonna go out and have some dinner and drinks. Then we're gonna strategize on how to get your boo thang back."

"Okay, I'm getting up now. Give me about an hour."

"Cool. See you then."

I got off the phone with Leah then drug myself out of bed. I ran myself a hot bath, turned on Keyshia Cole's, *Let It Go*, and turned on the jets in the tub and soaked.

Thirty minutes later, I was clean as a whistle and actually felt a little revived. I threw on some clothes, pulled my hair into a messy ponytail, and straightened up the house a little bit as I waited for Leah.

*Ding-Dong!*

Leah had arrived right on time. She gave me a hug as soon as I opened the door. "Hey hon, you ready?"

I wanted to just cry in her arms, but I took a deep breath, sucked it up, and put on a smile. "Yeah, I'm ready."

Leah tried to share words of inspiration as we headed to her car. "This isn't a pity party," she said. "We're preparing for a victory, you're gonna get your boo back."

We ended up at a bar not far from my house called Dudley's, which was the perfect atmosphere. We walked in and headed straight to the bar. Leah ordered our drinks as I got comfortable. Still a little shook from me and Black's heated argument, I cleared my mind and just relaxed.

"Oh, my god!"

"What is it?" Leah asked.

I stood up from my barstool and walked away immediately, totally ignoring her. It was like I was in a zone and no one or anything around existed as I headed toward the table in front of me.

"Well, I'm glad to see you're okay," I said. In my most sarcastic tone, my heart racing. This moment, and what I would do and say, had crossed my mind many times, but now that I was faced with it, I didn't know if I was ready for it.

Black didn't respond. He just looked up at me, disgust on his face.

"Hello? I'm talking to you. I was worried sick calling all over the place for you."

"I ain't have shit to say to you," Black said, looking down at his plate.

"You didn't have shit to say? I texted your ass nearly twenty times today. The least you could have done was let me know you were okay. Is that too much to fucking ask for Black?"

"I ain't have shit to say to you then, and I still don't have shit to say to you right now."

"What?" I wondered if this nigga had lost his fucking mind. Feeling disrespected, I began to get loud. "What you mean, you ain't got shit to say to me, Black? After all the shit we've been through, you really don't have shit to say to me?"

The chic that sat beside Black finally chimed in full of attitude. "Excuse me," she said. "I don't know if you noticed, but we're trying to have dinner here."

"Excuse me? No, excuse you." I responded, totally throwed off by this bitch's comment. "I noticed, but I just don't give a fuck. Who the fuck are you anyway? I don't know if you noticed, but I'm wearing a ring. I'm trying to have a conversation with my fiancé. Let me repeat that---fiancé." I spat back, feeling like I was about to explode.

"Fiancé? Well, he wasn't your fiancé when he was all up---. Oh, I almost forgot...neither was Swerve when you walked through the door and saw me sucking on his dick," the chic said.

Dazed, I stood motionless as the bitch's words registered in my head. This whole ordeal was hitting me like a fucking freight train, head-on and with no time to run for cover. I had to wonder how she had managed to get with both Swerve and Black. The realization sank in that my world was crumbling before my eyes.

It wasn't until I heard the chic say, "Fuck this! I'm out," that I snapped back to the moment.

"Yeah, bitch, that's the best thing for you. Be out!"

The chic stopped dead in her tracks, turned around, and stared me in the face.

"Or what?"

She was so close, I could feel the heat from her breath, for a moment I thought about getting out the pepper spray I carried in my handbag, but before I could do anything, I felt someone come between the chic and me.

"Or this." Leah tossed her drink all up in ol' girl's face.

"We'll cross paths again," the chic said. Knowing she was no match for me and Leah. She should have learned from the last ass whipping we gave her.

"Wait a minute, isn't that Yoshi," asked Leah.

"Yeah, that's that bitch."

I directed my attention back to Black, who was peeling out money from his wallet to pay for their meal.

"Oh, so you just gon' leave, Black? We are not gonna talk about this? You don't feel like you owe me an explanation or nothing?"

"I don't owe you shit. I just want to be by myself right now. I need some space. I'll be coming by the house to get my things." Black dropped a hundred-dollar bill on the table, then walked away, leaving me hanging.

"Yo, shortie, let's take a walk on the dock, I ain't ready to end our night like this," he said to Yoshi.

He gripped Yoshi by the waist and headed out the door.

## Chapter Twenty-Nine

"Hey baby!" Leah ran up and gave me a big hug and kiss.

"What's up? I see you really love daddy, huh? You came all the way around the globe to get your man. That's why I fuck with you so hard." I gripped her ass and pulled her close to me, my dick swelling.

"Damn! Looks like you're not the only one that's happy to see me," she said, feeling my dick stand up against her thigh.

"So, what you gon' do about that?"

"You'll see real soon. Get in the car. Let's get to the A."

"Oh, hey Bobby B, I didn't even see you," said Leah.

"I know you didn't. You got my boy's dick all up in ya eyes."

"Whatever," replied Leah.

I didn't hesitate to get in the car. Although I was horny as hell and wanted to fuck wifey more than anything, I can't lie my mind was on other shit. Everything in me wanted to meet up with D'Lamar, so I could give that nigga what he had coming to him.

We finally arrived in the A. After we dropped Bobby B off at his crib, Leah and I went to the house for some much-needed sex.

As soon as we got in the house, I wrapped my arms around Leah and began to kiss her passionately. My dick was so hard, it felt like it was going to explode. I turned around and pushed Leah against the wall, then put my hands inside her panties. Her pussy was hairless, and I instantly felt her swollen clit between her fat pussy lips.

"Ahhh, baby," she moaned. "Not right now". She pulled his hands from her panties.

I followed her to the bedroom. By the time we reached there, she was completely naked. I grabbed her naked body and tossed it on the bed.

"No baby, it's not time yet. First, you've got to get a shower."

Leah was trippin'.

"Hell nah. You 'bout to give me some pussy. I've been waiting for weeks for some pussy, and you gon' tell me to go take a shower first?

"Well, I'm getting in the shower. If you want me, you'll have to join me." She hopped up and ran into the bathroom.

I followed her in there. When I walked in, she was already in the shower. I ripped the curtain back and looked at her soaking wet perfect body. Although she'd had two kids for me, her body was still flawless, not a stretch mark in sight, I pulled off my clothes and got in with her.

As soon as I stepped in, she grabbed a washcloth and soaked it up. Then she began to wash my body from head to toe. Leah began to wipe me down, not missing one spot. I stepped under the flow of water to rinse the soap off.

When I turned around all of the soap was gone, Leah got on her knees and began to suck my dick. I knew I was backed up, so when I felt the need to come, I let the first one go and busted all in her mouth. Now that I'd gotten the quick one out of the way, it was time to really give it to her. My dick was still hard after I came.

I turned Leah around and bent her over under the flow of water beneath the shower head. I grabbed her by the waist and pushed my dick deep inside her.

"AAAHHHH, fuck!" she screamed out.

Her pussy was nice and tight like always. Water splashed off her ass as I banged it. Bouncing up and down turned me on even more. Before I knew it, Leah had reached her peak, and I followed shortly after. Although exhausted, we both washed off one more time before getting out of the shower.

Now that I broke wifey off with my good wood, it was time to break D'Lamar the fuck off.

I grabbed my iPhone and called him up.

"What up nigga?" D'Lamar sounded excited to hear from me.

"I'm on the streets nigga. Come scoop a nigga up."

"Yo, word, I'll be there in about 45."

"That's what's up," spat E-Love.

## **Chapter Thirty**

Yoshi and I took a walk on the docks, where no one was to be found. By this point the conversation had moved from Rhapsodee to more interesting things. It felt like only the two of us existed. A secluded area---the perfect setting for some bomb ass sex. For a moment I felt like Jamie Foxx and didn't know if I should blame it on the Henny or the Goose, but the more I looked at Yoshi, the sexier she became.

I kept making subtle passes and small flirtations with her. Although she resisted, I could tell, with a little more work, she would be dropping those jeans and lifting up her shirt, we made our way back to the bar. We stopped and talked for a minute outside while I finished up my cigarette.

"You know them?" Yoshi asked, pointing to a car that drove by slowly.

Unable to see who was in the car, I watched as they drove to the end of the parking lot and turned around. There was no one else in the parking lot other than me and her, so I figured they had to be watching one of us. A part of me wondered if Rhapsodee had hooked up with someone and decided to stalk a nigga. After all, the bitch was heated with me.

I took a long pull from my cigarette as I waited patiently for the car to come back around. The closer it got, the more I focused on the people inside. It wasn't until they'd gotten up on us again, that I'd realized the windows were tinted.

"Get--" I tried to warn Yoshi to get down, but before I could finish my sentence, shots had already rung out.

I jumped to the ground behind a car as I pulled out my gun. From there I shot back. I looked up to see Yoshi right beside me firing just as many shots.

"Come with me!" Yoshi, who was like a miniature Rambo, grabbed my arm and pulled me toward her truck.

Moments later, we were in her truck, and the people who were shooting after us had sped off.

"What the fuck was that?" Yoshi, asked, while catching her breath.

"I'm sorry ma, I feel real fucked up right now. I never meant to put you in danger like that. I had no idea."

"Danger? I love danger. It's kinda sexy."

Yoshi had my head fucked up with her response. "Oh yeah."

I wasn't a mind reader, but if I had to read her eyes, they were definitely saying, "I wish I could have a taste of that good dick."

"I don't think it's safe for us to go back in the bar. Can we go somewhere more comfortable?" she asked.

"Yeah, follow me to my crib," spat Black.

Yoshi readily agreed. "That's cool."

My mind was so fucked up. As I drove, I couldn't even think straight. If it wasn't for Yoshi picking up on that shit, I could have been fucked up.

Minutes later, we arrived.

Yoshi followed me through the door. Once inside, we got comfortable on the sofa.

"You okay, Black?" she asked, noticing the worry on his face.

"Just a little stressed out. This was an encounter with death. Worse, I could have gotten you killed. Basically, you're the reason I'm here. What the fuck you doing with a gun anyway? And where the hell did you learn to shoot like that?"

"First of all, don't worry about me. I've lived this life before. My brother is heavy into the drug game and I was ducking and dodging bullets and had to be on point every day."

Something about Yoshi's statement made me stop and think. What the fuck she mean into the drug game too? Who the fuck said I was in the drug game? I'd hoped no one ran their mouth to this bitch.

"I know it must be stressful." Yoshi stroked my face as she spoke to me.

"Stressful ain't the word ma. I've got beef coming in every direction, and on top of that, I don't even know if I can trust the chic, I was gonna make my wifey, right now I feel like it's me against the world. Real talk, for the first time, I was able to express the shit that had been on my mind.

"So, the chic, Rhapsodee, was your future wife?"

"Hold up, how do you know Rhapsodee?"

"Like she said…she caught me and her husband, Swerve, in the moment. I can almost imagine how she must be feeling."

"Hell nah," spat Black.

"Awww, you poor baby." Yoshi wrapped her arms around me and playfully kissed my cheek.

Seeing this as the perfect opportunity, I began to kiss her. And, just like that, she didn't resist. I slid my hand underneath her loose blouse and began to massage her breast. One touch of her nipple and my manhood rose to the occasion.

"Uummm," Yoshi moaned.

I gently laid her down, and she assisted me in taking her shirt off.

One by one, I sucked her breasts, while slowly sliding my hand into her panties. I had to be sure to make each move right. I didn't want to take the chance of her resisting and deciding not to go through with things.

Once my hands were in her panties. I buried my fingers deep between her fat pussy lips. Feeling the thickness and moisture alone of her pussy, made me want to bust. No longer able to resist, I pulled off my jeans, slipped on a jimmy, and before I knew it, I was all up that fat pussy I had been admiring earlier.

While slinging this big rod all up in her gushy stuff, she had the nerve to ask, "You got some work for me baby? I could use the extra money."

I kept beating that pussy up until I creamed all up in it. "Yeah, when you wanna start?"

# Von Diesel

## Chapter Thirty-One

I'd just gotten a call from E-Love to come pick him up. Truth be told, I was kind of disappointed that he had gotten out. I was enjoying being the king and running the castle.

I stopped by the gas station to fill up the car and to grab a six-pack of Corona for the road. I had a few in the car, but I needed to re-up just to get my mind right. As I walked in, there was a sexy little petite chic behind the register. I gave her a smile as I headed toward the freezer to get the Coronas. She smiled back. That's all I needed. I already knew I was gonna holla at her when I checked out.

I heard the lyrics of Miguel's song, *Pay Me*, blasting from a car stereo outside the store. Shortly after, I heard a commotion at the front of the store. It sounded like a group of rowdy niggas had just walked in.

"What's up, sexy?" One of the guys said, obviously speaking to the cashier at the front of the store.

Another one of the boys sang out the lyrics of Miguel's song. He sounded like he was getting closer to me.

Eager to get the fuck out of the store, I grabbed up the Coronas and headed to the front of the store. No sooner than I got to the end of the aisle, I caught eyes with one of the guys. He stood at the other end of the aisle. I followed him immediately. It was one of Flame's boys.

We locked eyes, like a cowboy standoff, and before I could blink, he fired a shot at me. One hit the case of Coronas, busting the bottles and causing them to drop out of my hand.

I dove to the next aisle and grabbed my gun. I met the guy at the front of the store, and we fired shots at one another, as his boy ran out the front door. Moments later, he followed behind him and jumped in the truck. I ran out the door after them.

On the way out, I noticed the cashier laid out on the floor, blood coming from her chest. She had been shot. I jumped in my car and followed the SUV Flame's boys were driving. I got up close enough to fire some shots. One shot hit a tire, almost sending the SUV out of control for a second.

I pressed the pedal to the floor, determined to catch up with them. As soon as I got by their side, the driver quickly busted a right turn and ended up losing control of the truck, which flipped over into the ditch.

I pulled over beside them. I saw the driver crawling from the truck and gave him two shots. I was sure that nigga wouldn't be breathing after this.

With no time to waste, I jumped back in my car and sped off, leaving no eyewitnesses behind. I had to make sure I put those niggas to rest, to let niggas on the street know what was really good. It took shit like that to get a name.

Now that I had a couple of murders under my belt, I was sure I would be respected on the streets. Money, power, and respect was all it took to be the boss. I had the money, and with money came power, and now I had finally gained the respect.

## Chapter Thirty-Two

"Got damn! What up, big homie?" I dapped up D'Lamar. "Take me straight to College Park," I said to him as I hopped in his car.

Once I was in College Park, D'Lamar would be easily dealt with. Then I would make up for that dough that his bitch ass fucked up.

"Man, how that shit happen again, on the real? How you fuck up the money?"

"Man, I hooked up with some of these other ATL cats. The first go 'round, I gave these niggas half of the shit, and everything went straight. The next time I met up with them to get rid of the rest, these niggas was on some other shit. They straight robbed me, man."

"What the fuck you doing dealing with them anyway? This why you got fucked up!"

"I know, but I could sell it to these niggas for a little more."

"Oh, so you were trying to make a little profit of your own. See where greed gets you? Nigga, you ain't ready to be no fucking boss, so stop trying to act like one!" I snapped.

"A'ight, dude." D'Lamar ended the argument.

The more I looked at D'Lamar, the angrier I got. I'd managed to deal with it nearly the entire drive, but that last few minutes was killing me. I was ready to take him out. I was waiting for the perfect opportunity.

"Yo, can you get a Corona for me off the back seat?" D'Lamar asked.

"Yeah," I replied, realizing this may be the opportunity I'd been waiting for. In jail, a nigga can get anything he wants. I was lucky enough to run into this dude that mixed up a number of prescription meds to make this drug that paralyzes you for at least six hours or so. It was the jail version of the street drug "Special K." Special K was actually a drug used to tranquilize cats.

I popped open a Corona for D'Lamar and put in a little of the drug and handed it to him. Pretending like I was concerned about D'Lamar drinking and driving, I suggested I take over the driving from that point.

"Man, I've been locking shit down while you were gone," he bragged.

"Oh yeah? How the fuck you lock shit down?" I knew this nigga was a little bitch and didn't have the balls to put a city on lock.

"Nigga, I knocked off Flame. Niggas thanking me this day. That nigga was going around taking niggas' money and drugs and shit. Ain't nobody has the balls to stand up that nigga. But I ain't back down. Instead, I made that nigga lay down."

"Yeah, I heard about that shit when I was locked up. I wondered what the fuck was going on."

"Nigga tried to bitch me out during a dice game, so I had to let that nigga know. Know what I mean?"

D'Lamar was going on like he really was the man on the streets.

"Right, right," I said, making him feel a little good.

"Then I got word that his boys were after me. Niggas was calling my phone, threatening me and shit, but I was like, *fuck it!* Y'all niggas know where to find me. I ain't hiding. So, days had passed, and I ain't never see none of these niggas, that is until tonight."

"Tonight? You ran into these niggas before you came to pick me up?" Now I was really interested in what D'Lamar had to say.

"Yeah man, I was at the fucking gas station, and these niggas rolled up on me. They started busting shots and shit, even hit the cute little cashier bitch. Anyway, I catch up with these niggas about a mile from the gas station. They had flipped the truck and shit, so when the nigga come crawling out the truck, I hit him with a couple of shots."

"So that nigga dead?"

Totally ignoring my question, D'Lamar called out in panic, "Yo, I can't move my legs."

That was my queue. It didn't even take ten minutes before that shit I put in his drink started to work.

"Pretty soon you won't be able to move your arms either." I gave him a devious grin.

"What did you do to me?"

"Shut the fuck up!" I yelled and punched him in his mouth. Afterwards, my hand hurt like hell.

Shortly after, we arrived at an abandoned warehouse I came across. I pulled D'Lamar's paralyzed body from the car and dumped it on the dirty warehouse floor. Then I placed duct tape around his arms and legs.

"What? You thought I was gonna let you get away at ducking me and playing with my fucking money? Not to mention, you violated me by putting your hands on my wife. That alone is a death sentence, bitch ass nigga. Did you forget where you came from nigga? You were nobody. I made you D'Lamar. When we met, you were on the corner selling nicks and dimes, nigga. I opened the doors for you!" I kicked him in the head. I couldn't believe this ungrateful ass nigga.

Having had enough of looking at this nigga any longer, I put my gloves on. And with his own gun, I shot him twice in the head and left him as a nice snack for the rats.

Now that I had one task down, it was time to move on the other.

# Von Diesel

## Chapter Thirty-Three

"So, look. I got a few deliveries you can take care of for me. One in Florida, the other in Alabama and the last just around the corner in Columbus.

"Oh, I got you."

"Cool. So, we'll set you up for Alabama first."

"A'ight den. Let's do this. Drive around to the side of the house."

I did just as Black had instructed and drove around the back.

Black brought out the packages of cocaine and told me to stand back. I almost fainted as I watched him take off the door panels of my new truck. I knew he had to hide the shit in a secure area, but just seeing the door panels off my truck like that, fucked me up.

Oh well, it's all part of the game. It'll be well worth it in the end, I thought as I looked on.

I knew in the end everything would end in my favor. That's one thing I always made sure of. My motto was, why settle for milk when you could have the whole cow? Why would I keep waiting for a handout, when I could easily do my own thing?

# Von Diesel

## Chapter Thirty-Four

E-Love and Black would be feuding in a couple of days. Yoshi was determined to play them against each other with the drugs. By the time Black found out the truth, Yoshi would be long gone with enough cash to last her a lifetime.

Determined to get the money, I used my only resource. I headed to the strip club, the Candy Shop. As an ex-stripper, I knew a lot of local as well as out-of-town drug dealers that hung out there.

Walking into the strip club, I didn't notice too many familiar faces. People would come and go all of the time. Stripping wasn't a line of work that exactly guaranteed job stability. One day you're there, the next day you're not. One day the money is good, the next day it's not. But even with all those downfalls, bitches still couldn't break away from the strip game. I guess it was the fast money that was so damn addictive. Just like niggas with the drug game, it was hard to let go.

"Creme, girl is that you?" A voice called out, addressing me by my ex-dancer name.

"It sure is," I replied back to Deja' and hugged her.

Deja' was a veteran of the strip game. She was actually the person responsible for my pole skills. She taught me how to work that pole in every way imaginable.

"How you been?" She asked, looking me up and down. "You coming back to work?"

"Don't you wish bitch," I thought. I knew exactly what was going through her head.

It wasn't unusual for a current stripper to an ex-stripper in such a manner. I knew she was looking for any signs that I was struggling or doing bad. When a chic stops stripping, other chics seem to think she has this, *I'm-better-than-you-attitude*. But in reality, the current strippers are jealous of the ex-strippers, because they wish they were in the other stripper's shoes and had the same opportunity to stop dancing themselves. So, if a chic happens to be one of those females that are fortunate enough to stop dancing and she comes in the strip club, the current dancer is always gonna be looking for something negative to say.

"I'm fine girl. Just dropping through. I'm not here for work." I put any suspicion that Deja' had to rest then switched the subject. "How's Keyonte' doing?"

"Next month he'll be seven."

Deja' pulled out her cell phone to show me the latest picture of her son. He was a real cutie with his front teeth missing. Looking at that picture instantly made me miss my boys.

"I'm glad I ran into you. I need a little bit of information and help."

"Whatcha' need, boo? You know I got your back."

"What I need to know is, where's the ballers at? Where's the niggas that's moving major weight around here?"

"See that nigga in the corner by the pool table? He goes by the name E-Love. That's one of the heaviest niggas that be coming to the club. That's who you want to get at."

Deja' assumed I was looking for a nigga to take care of me or to run some tricks with, but that was better for me. The less that bitch knew, the better.

"Thanks, girl. Do me a favor. Have the bartender send him over whatever he is drinking." I handed her a hundred-dollar bill.

I quickly went to the bathroom to look myself over and make sure my boobs were sitting up pretty and nice. Women would pay to have boobs like mine, but lucky me, I was just blessed with an awesome rack. Besides this fat cat, that was one of my greatest assets, and men couldn't keep their eyes off them.

After his drink arrived, E-Love looked around to see who sent him his bottle of Cîroc. I raised my matching glass to him and nodded my head, giving him a seductive smile.

After twenty minutes or so, I headed over to him.

"Hmmm. I'm a little impressed. I ain't never had a female buy me a bottle, or even a drink, as a matter of fact. And you are?" He smiled at me.

I gave him a fake name and grinned back at him. "My name is Kierra."

"It's nice to meet you, Kierra. So, what's up with you, little Momma?"

"Well, I got some birds that are ready to move, and worked on the street is, you the nigga I should be hollering at." I explained with much confidence, although inside I felt a little uneasy. Normally, I wouldn't take these types of chances, but I needed to get rid of Black's product, and fast. My back was against the wall.

"How much you want for them?"

We negotiated pricing. He got over a little, but a bitch was desperate, and anything was a profit for me, considering it wasn't my shit to begin with.

"A'ight den, it's settled. All I need to know is where and when?"

"In an hour, meet me in the parking lot of Stonecrest Mall, near AMC theater." I said, figuring that was a pretty safe place.

Von Diesel

## Chapter Thirty-Five

In thirty-minutes flat, Leah had arrived. I looked like a hot mess as I opened the door. I hadn't had the energy to do anything to myself. My normally long, thick, curly hair sat in a tangled mess on top of my head.

"Hey boo," Leah hugged me as soon as I opened the door.

"Hey, girl," I responded in my most desperate tone.

"Wow! You looked stress," Leah said, noticing my ragged look. "I know what you need right now."

"I need Black here with me right now, telling me we're still going to do the damn thing and get married. He acts like he doesn't even give a fuck about me. How can he treat me this way? It hurts to the core."

Leah stroked my tangled hair. "Everything will be alright."

I called those four words, *The Girlfriend's Anthem.* A true girlfriend sure could tell you that everything would work out, no matter how bleak shit looked.

"No, it won't," I said, seeing no light at the end of this dark, dark tunnel.

"Yes, it will, we're gonna get your man back," Leah said. "Now, this is what you're going to do."

"What?" I said between sniffles.

"You're going to first, get your ass out of the bed, take a shower, comb that nappy ass hair, then get dressed. We're going to Victoria Secrets and we're going to buy you some sexy negligee. You're going to cook his favorite meal and plan to have a romantic candle lit dinner."

"But I haven't heard from him in a week. How can I get him home?"

"You call him and tell him you want to talk. When he shows up, you let him be the man, and think everything is his idea, but then you screw his brains out."

"Oh God, I hope this works," I said, feeling hopeless.

"Hon, I know it hurts. I've been through this shit a time or two before myself. There aren't too many men who can say they've had my heart. I know you want Black back in your arms; it's what we both want. But right now, I'm going to get you a cup of herbal tea, so you can relax while you bathe."

Leah headed toward the kitchen and came back five minutes later with a cup of steaming hot tea.

"I took a sip. "Leah, this is good, girl." It soothed my scratchy throat.

"I Figured you would like it. I drink it when I'm stressed. Next, go get cleaned up so we can get going."

Once I got dressed, we headed out to the mall. "I pray this works," said a worried Rhapsodee.

## Chapter Thirty-Six

An hour came and went. I swear, muthafuckers didn't know the meaning of being on time. E-Love was running only ten minutes late, but each minute I waited felt like an eternity. I sat there nervous as hell and shaking. This should be a smooth transaction.

I saw a couple of guys pulling up next to me in a Yukon. I put one in the head and held the gun by my side, just in case some shit popped off. The two unknown guys stood by my driver and passenger door barricading it.

"What the hell is going on?" Before I could process anything, one of the guys was in my face.

"Roll the window down!" He ordered.

I refused to roll the window down as he instructed.

"Do what the fuck I say, and I won't blow your stupid ass up," he explained, holding up a grenade.

A grenade? This nigga can't be serious, I figured this had to be some type of joke. So, I yelled at him, "I ain't doing shit!"

He giggled. "Your ass will be blown to pieces."

I reached toward the gear shift to put my car in drive to pull off from this stupid-ass-nigga.

"Not so fast."

Bling!

Before I could react, my window was broken, and glass was shattered all over my face.

"Hey, Kierra, or should I say Yoshi," E-Love stepped in and greeted me.

I wondered how the fuck he knew who I really was. "I'm not Yoshi. My name is--."

E-Love cut off mid sentence.

"Yo, I'm not trying to hear shit you got to say, hand me over that bag."

"I am not giving you the drugs."

*Bam!*

E-Love punched me in the side of my face with one hand and pulled me out the window of the truck with the other. Then I felt the barrel of a gun pressed against my cheek.

Once my head stopped spinning and the stars before my eyes disappeared, I turned around to see a fucking AK in my face. That's when I started to realize this wasn't a joke at all. These niggas were literally ready for war, and I wasn't gonna put up a fight. I knew this would be a battle that I would lose. The thought of my sons was still fresh in my head.

"Put that shit up, nigga. Y'all couldn't wait for an opportunity to pull out the toys, huh?" E-Love barked. Y'all niggas don't need all that shit for this little bitch."

*BAM!*

I caught another punch to the face.

"Okay, Okay, I'll give you the bag!"

"See, all it takes is a little manhandling." E-Love laughed.

I struggled to my feet and headed toward the car. I opened the front door pretending I was going for the bag but grabbed my gun instead.

*CLAP!*

E-Love's boy hit me in the face with the butt of his gun. He'd obviously gotten a glimpse of me heading for my piece. "I told you this shit would come in handy," said Bobby B.

By the time blood was running down my face profusely, and my eyes were nearly swollen shut, I grabbed the bag and handed it to E-Love.

"I was hoping you would choose life." E-Love snatched the bag away from me. He quickly hopped back in his truck and sped away.

Karma's a real bitch. I shook my head in disappointment and exhaled. "Fuck you, Karma! You bitch!" I yelled out loud.

I grabbed some napkins out of the glove box and put them on my bleeding wound then put my car in drive and drove away empty-handed.

## Chapter Thirty-Seven

With Black on my mind, a fresh burst of energy told me to call him. I decided to do just as Leah had advised the night before and called Black.

"Yeah," Black greeted me on the phone after I dialed his number.

I was nervous as hell. I didn't want to take no for an answer of me seeing him.

"Hey baby," I said.

"Well, um, I was wondering if you could come over to the house for a bit. I just want to talk," I suggested, keeping my fingers crossed.

"I'll be over in a few hours. I need to get a few things anyway," he responded and hung up in my ear.

I didn't even care that he'd hung up on me. I was just happy he'd agreed to come over.

I ran to the store to get two fresh T-bone steaks and a few sweet potatoes to bake. I planned to smother them in apple butter, cinnamon and nutmeg, just the way Black liked it. Next, I planned to cut up a toss salad topped with French dressing and croutons. For dessert, it was going to be apple crumb cobbler.

Walking around in my black laced teddy and five-inch stiletto heels, gave me confidence. I felt sexy, like every man on earth wanted a piece of my pussy. I began to rehearse in my mind what I would say to Black, remembering to watch my tone. The last thing I wanted to do was get him mad and then have him storm off on me like the last time.

Von Diesel

## Chapter Thirty-Eight

"Oh my God Black!" I said, forcing out the words between fake cries.

"What's wrong?" Black yelled in panic.

I purposely didn't answer. I just continued to cry uncontrollably, to add more drama to my act.

"Yoshi!" Black yelled. "What the fuck is going on?"

"Some dude named E-Love robbed me. He beat me up and robbed me."

"What the fuck you doing with that nigga?"

"It's a long story. He tried to pull up on me at the gas station. He saw the bag on the front seat and snatched it while I was pumping gas.

"What? This nigga can't know that's my shit. Ain't no way he could fuck with my shit like that. Let me give that nigga a call."

He dialed E-Love's number three-way.

E-Love yelled into the phone as soon as he picked up, What up nigga?"

"What the fuck you doing taking my shit, nigga?"

"Fuck you talking 'bout, man?"

"Yoshi told me you robbed her. That's my shit!"

"Man, you believe that lying-ass bitch if you want to. Fuck her! And as a matter of fact, fuck you too for calling me with that bullshit. I got money nigga. I don't need your little-ass shit!" E-Love disconnected the call.

"Don't worry about shit," Black said to me. "I'll handle this shit with him. You all right, though?"

"I'm banged up a little, but I'll be okay." Black played right into my little plan. I must say, E-Love was right about one thing--- I was very conniving and believable.

"Cool. Call me if you need anything."

Von Diesel

## Chapter Thirty-Nine

Rhapsodee met me at the door, "Hey boo." She tried to kiss me on the lips, but I turned, and she caught my cheek instead.

While walking in the house, I was on my cell phone, talking to Sosa. I didn't know what Rhapsodee had in mind, but this one night wasn't gonna change how I felt about things between us.

I went into the kitchen to grab a Heineken from the fridge then glanced over at the food that she cooked. Damn! My favorite, I thought as my mouth began to water, but I refused to voice it. Instead, I acted like it didn't faze me.

I noticed Rhapsodee let out a big sigh, I guess to refrain from getting pissed and going the fuck off on me.

I grinned to myself and continued my phone conversation. "Yeah," I replied, walking over to the living room to sit down on the couch.

"Baby, how was your day?" Rhapsodee inquired.

"A'ight," I responded.

"Well, maybe I can make it end on a wonderful note." Rhapsodee began to massage my shoulders.

She poured vanilla-scented oil into her hands, rubbed them together to get the oil nice and warm, then caressed my shoulders deeply. I couldn't deny that shit felt damn good too.

"How's that?" Rhapsodee asked, after giving me a five-star full body massage.

"That was on point," I said, finally relaxed enough to notice how enticing her nightie was.

My dick began to rise as I watched Rhapsodee's ass bounce in her thong as she walked over to the bar to make me a Grey Goose on the rocks. I turned on the television and flipped through the channels, as I gulped down the drink she had made me.

"Uuummm…is this for me?" she asked, rubbing my now fully erect dick.

I didn't respond. I just gave her a grin and swallowed down the rest of the liquor I had in the glass.

Noticing my glass was empty, Rhapsodee immediately grabbed it and headed back to the bar to make me round two. This time before returning she turned on Jay-Z and Beyonce's, *Drunk in Love*, lit some candles and dimmed the lights. Upon returning to the couch, she took the remote from my hand and turned off the television.

As I sipped on my second glass of Grey Goose, Rhapsodee slipped off my pants. She grabbed my dick and started to lick the tip of my head, gently getting it nice and moist. Then she moved down the shaft, licking it up and down a couple of times, then continuing to my balls, a tingling sensation filled my body as she engulfed my balls in her mouth at one time.

By this time, my dick was so hard, it felt as though it was gonna explode. Just when I thought I couldn't take it anymore, Rhapsodee grabbed my dick and began deep-throating it just the way I liked it. I spread my legs, grabbed a handful of her hair, and pushed her face deep in my lap. I closed my eyes and let my head fall back as I absorbed each second of this goodness. One thing for sure, there was no denying that Rhapsodee gave a hell of a blowjob.

"You like that?"

"Suck that shit, bitch!" I grabbed Rhapsodee's hair even tighter, forcing her head down farther onto my rock-hard dick.

"Aaaahhh fuck!" Rhapsodee started to gag as my cum rushed out the tip of my dickhead and hit the back of her throat. She sucked off every drip and swallowed like she was eating her favorite ice-cream.

That shit was just foreplay to me. I grabbed Rhapsodee and ripped her lingerie off. I pinned her to the carpeted floor and forced three of my fingers into her soaking wet pussy.

"You give my pussy to another nigga?"

"No, baby, you know this is yours."

"Maybe you giving this ass up." I forced my thumb in her ass. She screamed out in pain. "AAHHH! No, baby. No, I'm not!"

Instead of sucking on her nipple, I bit it. There was no fucking love making this night. To make love, you had to be in love, and honestly, I felt no love for her at the time. The thought of her betraying me for my half-brother killed the feelings of love I had for her.

"Ahhh shit!" Rhapsodee cried out. "Black, you're hurting me, baby."

I pushed in even deeper and harder as I began to reach my peak. "Take the dick, Rhapsodee."

"Baby, please pull out. Don't cum in me, Black."

"Where you want it? You gonna take it on your titties or on your ass?"

"Wherever you want, baby. Just pull it out."

"Aaaaaahhhhh!" After I banged the pussy up DMX's style as in the movie *Belly*, I came deep inside her, totally ignoring her request to pull out.

"Black, you came in me?" She asked, feeling my wetness drip from inside her.

"Yep," I said as I jumped up.

I quickly headed upstairs. I wasn't trying to hear that shit Rhapsodee was talking. If it was my pussy like she had just claimed minutes earlier, then I was free to do whatever I liked with it.

I jumped in the shower and freshened up, then headed to the bedroom and grabbed some clothes. I made sure I packed enough things to last me for a while. I didn't want to make another trip back over to the house anytime soon.

"Where are you going?" Rhapsodee asked.

I guess me packing and leaving wasn't in keeping with her plans. "Back to my crib," I told her. "I'm out!"

"We haven't talked yet."

"Like I said, I'm out," I repeated, and turned to leave.

Rhapsodee ran into the kitchen and grabbed the two plates of food that she had prepared while I was in the shower. "Don't forget your dinner!" She threw the two plates of food up against the wall near where I was standing.

I didn't give a fuck, as long as she didn't hit me. I heard her on the phone as I continued to gather my last few items.

"Hello, Leah," she said between sobs. "He's leaving."

Not wanting to be a part of the drama, I rushed out the door, slamming it behind me.

Now I see why Swerve wanted that bitch dead…she always in a muthafucka' business. What she needs to be doing is gettin' my money from the fuck nigga as husband she got, before I blow his ass to pieces.

Rhapsodee was a dumb hoe. Bitch can't even keep her business to herself, this why she ain't got no man now, as Black thought to himself as he drove away.

## Chapter Forty

"Yo," I answered Sosa's call hoping he was gonna deliver the message I'd been waiting for.

"I spotted Yoshi, she's on her way to the Candy Shop.

"Cool. I'm on my way."

I'd waited nearly two weeks to find this bitch... "Jackpot!"

I jumped in my car and headed to the club, where I slid in unnoticed, trying to draw as little attention to myself as possible.

The scene was the same as the very first time I'd gone there. There was a group of guys in one corner playing Madden on the projector screen, another set gambling in another corner, and Sosa was in another spot, having a conversation with another cat.

I entered the dice game. After about fifteen minutes, I heard niggas talking about a fat ass that just bounced into the club, so I turned around to check out that ass too.

*Bingo!* I thought, a smile spreading across my face. That fat ass looked real familiar to me. I was almost certain it belonged to Yoshi.

To be sure, I pulled out my cell phone and scrolled down to her name then hit send. Moments later, her phone began to ring, and she started to fumble through her purse to search for it. Already having my confirmation, I hung up.

I sat quiet as a mouse, watching Yoshi's every move. She didn't look in the direction of the dice game, so she didn't even notice me.

When I saw her leave the club, I slipped out of the club and cautiously made my way to the car and jumped in. I noticed Sosa right behind me.

We spotted Yoshi loading the duffle bag Black had given her from the back seat to the trunk of her car. We waited until she left the parking lot and followed her for more than twenty minutes, waiting for the right time to let her have it.

"Looks like she's headed to her crib," Black said. "We gotta be careful because she got two little shorties living there."

I watched as she pulled onto a quiet neighborhood street then into an apartment complex. Yoshi grabbed her duffle bag and headed into her third-floor apartment.

Minutes later, we grabbed our guns and rushed to her apartment. I kicked the door in. I was the first to spot her. "Surprise, surprise, Bitch!' I said, pointing the gun in her face.

"What the fuck is this?"

*Smack!*

I hit her hard in the face with the gun, and she dropped to the floor.

"Shut the fuck up, bitch!" Sosa pinned her to the living room wall. "I ought to kill your muthafuckin' ass."

I punched her in the face. "How long did you think you were going to keep playing us and we not figure out your damn scheme?" This bitch deserved to get beat like a dude. She thought she was so fucking slick, taking other people's money.

Sosa still had her pinned to the wall. "Please...my sons are in the other room sleeping. Don't hurt them," she begged, almost breathless.

"Let her go," I ordered Sosa, and she felt helpless to the ground, choking, and trying desperately to catch her breath. "I got something better in store for you bitch." I snatched her shirt off, leaving her in her bra.

"You want to see what it feels like to have something precious taken from you?" I slid my gun beneath her bra, forcing her breasts to pop out.

Yoshi tried desperately to crawl away. "Please don't do this."

Wham! I kicked her one time in the stomach.

As she balled up in the fetal position, I lifted her skirt and began to unbutton my pants. I was gonna teach her a lesson.

I glanced over to see Sosa standing in the corner like a scared little bitch.

I forced her legs open. My dick was rock-hard as I slid her panties off, leaving her completely naked.

"Mommy," a little boy called out, rubbing his eyes.

Without flinching, I shot him in the leg one time.

"No, not my baby! Nooo! He didn't deserve that!" Yoshi screamed out, trying to fight with all her might.

Now that shit had turned in a different direction, sex was no longer a priority. I needed to get the money and get the fuck out. Besides, Sosa looked as if he was gonna pass out at any moment.

I kicked Yoshi in the stomach again. "Where's the money?"

"My baby!"

"Where's the fuckin' money?" I followed with three more kicks to the stomach.

"Oh my God!"

"Where's my muthafuckin' money, bitch?" I punched her in the head to help her remember where it was.

"All right, all right, I will get it for you. It's in the living room closet," she informed us and began slowly crawling in that direction.

Sosa and I quickly went to the living room and opened the closed door. We began to search through all the shit stacked up in the closet.

"It's near the back," she said between tears.

After ransacking the closet for a few minutes and still not finding shit, I started to feel this bitch was trying to play me. I turned around, planning to go and shoot this bitch's other son, to let her know this shit wasn't a game, but to my surprise, when I turned around, she was gone.

I looked up just in time to see her climbing over the balcony. I started firing shots, and this crazy bitch straight jumped, never looking back or thinking twice.

Sosa and I rushed over and looked from the balcony of the apartment to see a lifeless body covered in blood. I would have shot that bitch again, but from the looks of things, there was no need. That bitch was definitely gone, her body twisted like a pretzel and blood flowing all around her.

Almost instantly, people started to crowd around her and yell out for help. The last thing my ass needed was even more witnesses to get rid of. Sosa and I got the fuck out of there. This shit was spiraling out of control. We ran down the stairs, but when we reached the bottom, police were already pulling up. There was no way we could make a run for it. Knowing Sosa would only slow me up, I dipped off, leaving him alone. He didn't even resist, and the cops arrested him right away.

The cops were right on my heels.

"Get down! Put your weapon down!"

There was no way I could go down. This time for sure I would never see daylight. With no option left, I decided to shoot my way out. It was do or die.

I stopped in my tracks, turned around, and faced the cops. They all froze and pointed their guns right at me. I said a silent prayer and slowly lifted my gun.

*BAM! BAM! BAM! BAM!*

It seemed like shots rang out forever, my body gyrating and burning all over. I knew I was taking my last breath, and this was lights out.

## Chapter Forty-One

I was disappointed with myself. I was usually on point with shit, but I had to admit, I'd fucked up a whole lot in these past few weeks. I was on my way to get one of those prepaid cell phones to conduct my business, but first I needed to pay E-Love a visit.

It worked out in my favor that I spotted him at this lil' strip club called *Bottoms Up*, that I frequented. The last time I ran into him, it was at that same spot.

I discreetly sat in the corner of the club and waited patiently for an hour for him to head out.

I watched him stagger to his truck. I pulled out of the parking lot behind him. He was too drunk to realize I was even following him. Plus, I was thankful he didn't have Bobby B with him. The less witnessed, the better for me. Besides, the only one whose head I wanted to put a bullet in was E-Love's.

E-Love pulled up in his garage. Just as he was closing the garage door, I literally rolled my body in underneath it before it shut. When I pressed up on him, his back was turned.

"Nigga, what the fuck you doing here?" He asked before I put my gun into his back.

"You don't get to ask any questions without warning," I shot him in the leg.

"Man, you shot me!" He whimpered in surprise.

"Do we understand each other? Next time I have no problem with shooting you in the throat."

"Yeah, I got you." He nodded, sweat coming from his forehead.

"Take me to your basement." I shoved him in the back with my gun.

I followed a limping E-Love through his house and into his basement. Once there, I tied him up with some tape he had on the counter in his basement and got ready for his execution.

"Black, man, please don't kill me," he begged. "I got kids."

"There you go again with your mouth." I pistol-whipped him.

"Please," he said, blood pouring down the side of his face.

"Why you think I stole from you, bitch nigga? I run these fucking streets. You really think I need to steal from you?" E-Love asked.

"Yoshi told me you robbed her. That shit was worth eighty grand."

"Man, I ain't rob that bitch. I found out that bitch tried selling yo shit to them niggas out in Lithonia. I guess she set us both up, man. That bitch is grimy. Maybe she was hoping one of us would be in a six-feet-deep grave right now. Please!"

"Nigga, shut the fuck up! Crying like a little bitch!" I untied him enough where he could maneuver his way out of the ropes. Then I quickly dipped out of his crib.

I knew deep down inside this nigga was telling the truth. One, I knew how this bitch Yoshi moved, and two, just how that shit happened didn't seem right. First, the bitch wanted my dick. Then when I gave it to her brought about the perfect opportunity for her to make some cash and rob me at the same damn time. Little do she know, she 'bout to pay the piper. And now I'm on some get-back type shit, cause of that funky ass lie she told. I just shot my boy. I had to be on my game. I took advantage of that nigga because he was drunk. E-Love is a natural born killer, and that alone tells me that I can't get caught slippin' with my weapon on safety.

## Chapter Forty-Two

I sat in the car watching Yoshi's apartment, waiting to see Black and Sosa emerge. I was so close to Black and I wasn't going anywhere until I'd brought justice to the muthafucka's who put a hit out on Swerve.

I cringed at the way his lifeless body was before me that day at the jail, laying in a pool of blood. I had never seen anything so horrific.

"What the hell?" I asked myself as I heard a gunshot, and then seeing a young woman jump from the third floor of the apartment building.

People were running and screaming from everywhere.

I exited my car and ran over with the crowd to the body. I covered my mouth when I saw that it was Yoshi.

I ran back to my vehicle and grabbed my 45. As I made my way to the apartment building, I heard sirens. Police cars were coming from every direction. I ducked between two bushes and threw my weapon over a tall fence.

Next thing I know, Black and Sosa ran out of the apartment building in an attempt to get away. Sosa didn't have a fighting chance, because he ran with a limp. Black being the bitch he was, started firing shots at the police. He managed to escape without one single bullet wound, leaving Sosa behind to take the fall.

As Sosa was being handcuffed and hauled away, I had managed to come from hiding. I walked over to the detectives and asked what happened, showing concern. I saw a female detective walk out of the apartment building with a young boy in tow and an infant in her arms. I walked over to her in tears and said, "The young woman that jumped was my grandchildren's mother. I can take them from you."

"Are you the victim's mother?" asked the officer.

"No, I'm their father's mother," Dorothy Smith-St. John, everyone in the hood calls me, Momma D."

As I made my way to my vehicle, the detective said, "Ma'am, don't forget the car seats, we found them in the victim's apartment.

Here's the baby's diaper bag. I loaded it with formula and diapers. Also, could I please see some identification?"

"Uh, yes officer," I said as I reached in my purse for my identification.

"Just wait in your vehicle for a few minutes, we have someone from the Department of Family Services that needs to ask you a few questions."

"Okay officer, we'll be right here."

After speaking with the Department of Family Services, I drove away and parked across the street at a nearby elementary school. After everyone had left the scene, I double-backed and retrieved my .45 from across the fence. Getting back in the car, I contemplated my next move.

"One phone call will not hurt," I said. I picked up the phone and slowly dialed her number, silently hoping that she would answer.

"Hello?" the young woman answered.

"Is this Rhapsodee St. John?"

"Yes, it is."

"You don't know me, but I'm…"

## Chapter Forty-Three

After my little incident with E-Love, I had to get out of Atlanta. I couldn't believe I escaped the shootout with the police at Yoshi's without any bullet wounds. I was lucky to have made it out alive. I have to admit, shooting E-Love in his leg was a wrong move. I knew that nigga wasn't gonna rest until I was six feet under.

I had been driving for what seemed like an eternity. Looking down at my watch, the clock read a little after 2 a.m. Travelling down 65-South was easy and smooth as a muthafucka'. I almost fell asleep at the wheel. The last time I dozed off, I veered to the left and woke up in time to barely miss the deep ridges on the side of the road, which scared the hell out of me. One thing for sure, those things definitely worked. Otherwise, my ass would have come off the highway and ended up in the ditch.

I turned on some rap music and rolled down every window in my truck as I continued to drive.

My plan was to go chill at Papa Doc's for a while and lay low. I needed to get my mind right and sort some things out. I called him up to run things by him.

Out of my left rear view mirror, I noticed this black Tahoe had been following me ever since I'd passed Auburn University. At that time, I was almost to Montgomery. It wasn't unusual for a person to be behind you for a while, because 65-South was such a long stretch, but I didn't want to take any chances.

I pressed on the gas pedal and moved up the eighty miles per hour. The Tahoe did the same. I moved up to ninety and hauled ass. When I said they were still keeping up, I was sure I was being followed. I pulled out my gun and cocked it.

I slowed down a little, prepared to bust shots all up in that fucking truck, but to my surprise, as soon as I slowed down, sirens began to go off. I looked in the rearview to see blue and red flashing lights on the dashboard of the truck. It was the fucking police in an unmarked car!

My forehead was sweating, and my heart felt as though it was beating out of my chest, but I couldn't lose focus. I continued to keep my eye on the Tahoe and on the road.

I moved up to ninety-five miles per hour. I wasn't going to let those fucking pigs take me in without a fight and throw me in a urine-infested cell. I drove like a crazed man, swerving around cars.

In no time, I was in Montgomery. I knew a few spots I could definitely dodge the fucking police in that area, especially since it was only one truck after me.

I didn't know if this nigga thought he was "super cop" or what, but he never called for backup. Shit like that made me think they wanted to do a nigga in. With no backup, he could kill me and then say it was in self-defense. You could never tell when it came to the cops these days.

I noticed an exit ramp a short distance ahead. I hopped on the ramp. Doing ninety, not letting up on speed the least little bit.

Just as I was going around the curve on the ramp, I looked up to see a fucking Honda Accord coming the wrong way. It was coming right at me. With no time to stop I swerved to avoid hitting it.

Unfortunately, the black Tahoe behind me wasn't so lucky. All I heard was a loud crash, then I saw the Tahoe go up into the air and flip over at least five times. Then the Tahoe rolled and landed with the tires up.

"Damn!" That nigga gotta be good as dead. My next stop was the NOLA, to see Papa Doc.

## Chapter Forty-Four

On the way home, Princess rehearsed her "*I'm leaving you*" speech over and over again. It was gonna be hard to face Marcus without trying to claw his fucking eyes out, but at this point, it was whatever, she thought.

Her cell phone started ringing, but no number registered on the screen. She debated for a moment on whether she should answer it.

"Hello?" she finally answered.

"Yo, Princess, they got me locked up," said Seven.

"What?" Princess had been caught off guard.

They raided the Candy Shop last night. I had your shit on me and got locked the fuck up. I'm at Fulton County, so ante up and get me out. My bail is five thousand."

"A'ight, I got you," Princess said nonchalantly.

Damn, what next?

"I hope so, because if you have me here for too long, I'ma start talking." Seven hung up before Princess could respond.

When Princess walked in the apartment, Marcus was on the phone, but her anger toward him was now diverted toward getting that bitch Seven out of jail. She cut her eyes at him as hard as she could to let him know they had beef, while passing him to get to the bathroom.

"Yo, K'Dub, my chic stays mad at me, dawg," Marcus said, noticing her attitude.

Princess slammed the bedroom door. She despised K'Dub's ass too. Plopping down on the foot of the bed, she tossed her car keys to the side and just sat for a moment, thinking about Seven's threat to snitch her out. The more she contemplated, the more she realized that Seven ain't have nothing on her, but her stage name. She didn't know her real name, or where she lived, or anything about her connect. She was no longer worried.

If I was a complete bitch, I'd let her ass hang, Princess thought, getting up and walking over to the closet for her stash. She could still hear Marcus on the phone with K'Dub. When she heard Twin's name being mentioned. she pressed her ear against the door, eavesdropping on what Marcus was saying.

"Who, Twin?" asked Marcus. E-Love was wrong for that shit. Hell, he was fucking around with her a couple of months before he went after Leah."

"Shit," K'Dub remarked, "I don't think Leah even knows, man. It's fucked up how they be skinning and grinning up in each other's faces."

"You think he's still digging on Twin?" asked Marcus.

"What?" quizzed K'Dub. "I think so."

"Come on man, the nigga tried to kill her," spat Marcus. Yo, that's your boy."

"Nah, I can't even fuck with him no more".

Yeah, he be bugging the fuck out," replied K'Dub.

"Anyway, what's up with that money? I got mine ready nigga. I'm waiting on yours," said Marcus.

Princess directed her attention down the Timberland shoebox, she noticed that it felt extremely light. Princess opened the box and instantly noticed the dent in her savings. What used to be 44 G's was now only three thousand dollars.

Princess threw the shoebox on the floor, dug in the back of the closet, pulled out one of those metal baseball bats, and stormed out into the living room.

"Where the fuck is my money at, huh?" she screamed.

"Whoa, whoa! Yo, nigga I'ma hit you back." Marcus quickly hung up the phone. "Aye yo, Princess, chill the fuck out!" he yelled, making a move to grab the bat. Princess stepped back and swung with all her strength, hitting his arm.

"Don't fuck with me, Marcus. Where the fuck is my money, you dirty-dick nigga."

"Yo, what the fuck is wrong with you, girl?"

Princess positioned herself to slug his ass again.

"Yo, chill! Don't hit me no more!" he ordered, as if he was in any position to make any demands.

"Marcus, I swear on everything I love, if you don't give me my money right now, I'm gonna take this fucking bat and try to kill you with it."

"Princess, listen. I just need a couple of weeks. Let me make this move with K'Dub and I promise you, I'll give you back double. Come on ma, put the bat down. Just grind with me, please, so I can get this paper, a'ight? Come on, baby, you know I got you. Jay-Z can't shine without his Beyonce."

Princess did the math. Double meant eighty-thousand grand. She weighed out her options.

*Seven's bail or a forty-thousand-dollar profit. Fuck Seven,* she thought, lowering the bat.

"See, that's why I love you, girl." Marcus let out a hard sight of relief.

Princess turned up her lips and gave him a "whatever" nigga look.

"Well, if you love me like that then go get your dirty-dick cured and stop fucking them nasty-ass hoes." She walked back in the bedroom, slamming and locking the door behind her. Princess lay on the bed, trying hard to understand how and why she loved Marcus's grimy ass so much.

Von Diesel

## Chapter Forty-Five

"Jayden Sosa, you have the right to remain silent. Anything you say can and will be used against you in a court of law. You have the right to an attorney...the officer read me my Miranda rights.

Yeah, yeah, yeah. Fuck you and Miranda! And that can go on record," I snapped as they lifted me from the ground and directed me to the cop car. The ride to Fulton County Jail was long and uncomfortable. I sat slumped sideways, with my hands still cuffed, in the cramped backseat of the police car. I actually was relieved when we reached the station. I was ready to just get this whole ordeal over with.

From the car, I was escorted straight to the interrogation room and left freezing like a piece of meat in a freezer. I sat alone for forty-five minutes, shivering in this small room with nothing but a table and three chairs. I never quite understood the purpose of having the room below zero or the purpose of leaving you in the room alone for so long.

Finally, a man walked in who introduced himself as detective Willis. Almost to the point of going stir crazy, I welcomed the tall, husky, ball-headed white man, who seemed like he should have been playing some sort of contact sport instead of being a detective.

"Jayden Sosa, you're being charged with murder and first-degree assault," the detective said as my mine wandered elsewhere.

What the fuck? Murder and assault? My first reaction was one of disappointment, but the I really thought about what was being said to me. I'm going to prison, and I'm never getting out. My heart palpitated, and I felt dizzy as I registered exactly what this man was telling me. I didn't murder or assault anybody. These wasn't my charges, and I wasn't wearing that shit for nobody.

"Do you understand your rights and the counts you are being charged with?" The detective asked.

I'd missed all the information he'd said in between and although I was still in shock, I just answered, "yes sir".

"Now, I know you're not a bad person Sosa. You're the father of a five-year-old son, and I know you need to be out there with him. So, I'm here to help you."

I knew the detective was lying. He didn't give a fuck about me or my kid. I'd seen this same scenario one too many times on the A&E series, the First 48. I knew what was coming next. He wanted me to help him, and he would help me.

I played along, "Please don't take me away from my son," I pleaded.

"Well, here's the thing. We know we have enough information to charge you. That's no question. The little boy was shot at, but luckily the bullet missed him. That first-degree assault could be dropped to child endangerment. Yoshi is dead. So, you're looking at murder. And you'll probably never see your son again. I don't want that to happen to you, so I'm willing to help you, if you're willing to help me."

The detective gave almost the same spiel I'd heard on the First 48 time and time again. It was almost comical. I had to wonder if that was a speech all cops learned in the academy.

"So, what do I have to do?" I asked, continuing to play along.

Detective Willis laid out the deal. "There's a major drug ring in Atlanta that revolves around you, E-Love, Black, Bobby B and Cadillac Dave. And we know you were longtime friends with Black. So, what information can you give us to bring down their operation? Your cooperation in helping us bring them down can determine the outcome of your charges.

Seeing this as the perfect opportunity to kill two birds with one stone--getting out of jail and getting a reduced charge, I readily agreed. I despised Black's ass for leaving a nigga behind to take the rap. If he found out I manipulated half of his product from Yoshi, I don't know how safe a nigga would be out there on the streets.

"Okay, I'll tell you what I know," I told him. E-Love was the main man. He brought cocaine from Miami and flooded the city. Black was his right-hand man, and together they were killing the drug game. Money constantly flowed, but when E-Love got busted this last time in Miami, Black stabbed him in the back and stole all of his customers.

The detective continued to fish for information. "Do you have phone numbers, addresses, or can you give us any other people that may be involved in this ring?"

Careful to tell the detective just enough to ease his hunger, but not enough to incriminate myself, we had a deal. By the end of our interrogation session, I had told detective Willis what I wanted him to know and submitted a written statement.

When it was all said and done, I'd given detective Willis what he wanted, and we had a deal. I ended up being charged with child endangerment, but in return, I would have to testify against Black once he was arrested. Neither one of us was to blame for Yoshi's death, because the bitch jumped over the balcony and killed herself, and as far as her son was concerned, he was never even shot. I knew that we both were innocent. I just manipulated the system to get out. Besides, they could care less about Yoshi being dead or her bitch-ass son being shot or shot at for the matter. They were only concerned with the drugs. I can't lie, this shit made me nervous as hell, but a nigga had to do what he had to do to save his ass.

Von Diesel

## Chapter Forty-Six

E-Love knew he had to get to the hospital as he tried his best to drive with his left leg. The pain that vibrated in his right leg was excruciating and he felt as if he would pass out at any minute. There was blood all over the front seat of his truck. He pulled into the first parking space he saw, nearly crashing as he pulled up to the hospital.

He opened his car door with blood all down the left side of his body. His face felt as if it would explode from the blows that Black had delivered. He spit blood out of his mouth as he yelled for someone to help him. Two nurses came rushing out of the hospital. They put him in a wheelchair and immediately rushed him into the emergency ward.

"He's lost a lot of blood!" He heard someone shout. As they wheeled him into an operating room, E-Love went into shock.

"We need to get him stabilized," yelled the attending physician. E-Love watched helplessly as the doctor filled him with anesthesia. "Sir, can you tell me your name?" E-Love slowly opened his mouth. "E-Love...I mean, Eric...Langford."

The doctor held up his fingers. "Okay, Eric. I want you to count all the fingers that I have in front of me. We have just given you an anesthetic that will put you to sleep." E-Love began to count, but before he could get to three, he drifted off into a mind-numbing sleep.

After two hours of surgery, E-Love woke up in a dark hospital room. He didn't have enough energy to sit up and look around. All he could do was move his eyes. He was groggy and the pain in his leg was better than before, but still painful by any standard.

A nurse entered the room and opened the blinds. The sun felt as if it were burning out E-Love's eyes. He shaded his eyes with his hands and weakly said, "While I'm here, could you keep the blinds closed and the lights out?"

The nurse just nodded her head, closed the blinds and exited the room. A couple minutes later, a doctor came in.

"Mr. Langford, you gave us quite a scare." E-Love just smiled, and the doctor continued. "Well, we were able to remove the bullet from your leg, but it chipped pieces of your bone. You probably feel sharp pains running up and down the sides of your leg. This is because the bone needs to heal itself before you will be able to walk again."

E-Love couldn't believe what he was hearing. He didn't even know how to respond to what the doctor was telling him.

"Now, it won't take long to heal, but give it a couple of weeks. And even then, you will have a slight limp because the bone in your right leg will not be as sturdy as the bone in your left leg."

"Your face will be sore for about a week or two. It was bruised pretty badly. We also gave you five tiny stitches above your left eye. We have prescribed some pretty heavy medications that should reduce the amount of pain that you are in. We're going to keep you for a couple of days, and if you need anything, just press that red button by the side of your bed."

He looked at him for a minute to let him absorb everything he had just told him. "Do you have any questions?" he finally asked.

E-Love shook his head. He was exhausted both mentally and emotionally.

I can't stay here for a couple of days. I've got to pay Black back with his life.

E-Love tried to sit up, but he was too weak. His head pounded and he felt nauseated. He realized he might have to stay for a day or two since he really couldn't even move. He tried to make himself as comfortable as possible, before he drifted into a fitful sleep.

The next morning, E-Love woke up to a dark room. He was glad that the nurse had followed his instructions and not opened the blinds. He reached for the buzzer to ask for help going to the bathroom. When he got no response after about five minutes, he grew irritated, knowing they must have heard the damn buzzer by now. He kept pressing for another few minutes then decided to try and make it to the bathroom by himself, thinking it was only a few steps away.

He struggled to sit up in the bed, after failing, he realized he could just raise the electric bed to sit himself up. He swung his good leg over the side and gently eased upon the leg that had been shot. As soon as his leg hit the floor, he winced in pain.

He took a deep breath and slowly guided himself along the wall. When he reached the bathroom, he searched for the light switch. He couldn't find it and became frustrated, but he had to go. He went into the dark bathroom.

After E-Love used the restroom, he sat on the toilet to rest his injured leg for a minute. While he was sitting, he heard the door to his room open. Just as E-Love was about to yell for the nurse to help him out of the bathroom, he heard three muffled gunshots.

E-Love froze and held his breath, fearing that whoever was in his room would hear him in the bathroom. E-Love's eyes widened in horror as he heard footsteps. When they stopped outside the bathroom door, E-Love searched for something to defend himself with. To his relief, the intruder left the room and E-Love was able to breathe again.

He stumbled out of the bathroom, not caring that his leg was injured. The only thing he was thinking about was getting the fuck out of there.

He limped to the standby his bed and grabbed his keys. When he glanced at the bed, he noticed the time bullet holes where his body would have been. He limped as quickly as possible out of the room.

E-Love snuck down the halls of the hospital painfully but swiftly. When he got to the parking lot, he realized he didn't know where he had parked his truck. He looked around the lot, and when he didn't see it, he pressed the alarm button on his key ring.

He heard his truck beep in the back of the lot. He struggled to get to his vehicle, and his leg ached with each step. When he finally made it, he collapsed into the front seat. He was relieved to be off of his leg, but he knew he couldn't sit still for too long. Paranoia swept over him as he put his truck in drive and headed to his house.

# Von Diesel

## Chapter Forty-Seven

Princess stared at the ceiling half of the night, tossing and turning. Seven's threats, her STD results, Marcus's infidelity, and her money investment with him, were all too much to grasp. Through it all, one thing troubled her the most---Marcus's phone conversation with K'Dub earlier. Despite every nerve in her body--plus, she had enough problems of her own not to get involved in someone else's--she knew her conscience would only eat away at her if she kept quiet about it. Not only did she feel Twin had every right to know what really went down, she also felt, without a doubt, that E-Love's mysterious running partner, "Hershey," should pay for his actions.

Princess glanced at the clock on the nightstand, which read 12:45 a.m. She got out of the bed, still fully dressed from earlier. Without turning on the lights, she felt around the bed for her car keys, which were still at the foot of the bed where she had left him.

She unlocked and slowly opened the bedroom door. Peeking out, she saw Marcus, asleep on the couch, with the TV watching him.

Thank God, she thought. The last thing she wanted to hear was his mouth.

Princess left the house, went for a drive, and ended up in front of Twin's apartment. She called her on the cell.

"Hello?" Twin answered.

"What's up, Twin? I need to holla at you about something."

"Who's this?"

"It's Princess. Come outside."

"Princess, I'm sleeping."

"Twin, E-Love ain't do it."

"What?" Twin's voice got louder.

"E-Love ain't the one that shot you, but since you are sleeping, fuck it."

"No, wait. I'm coming." Twin was awake now. She hung up, hopped out of bed, threw on some sweats and slippers, and headed out the door.

Opening Princess's passenger-side door, she got in, eagerly anticipating what she had to say.

"What's going on, Princess?"

"Listen, I know who shot you. I don't know him like that, but he be with Marcus and this guy named K'Dub."

"Well, who is he and how is he linked to me?"

"His name is Hershey. He used to run with E-Love."

"So, how do you know he's the one who shot me?" asked Twin.

"Look, that's not important. I just know, okay."

"Marcus's boy, K'Dub is feeling you hard, so I was thinking maybe you should fuck with the niggas just to manipulate the situation, try to turn him against Hershey. That way he could take care of him for you, Princess suggested.

"I don't know. I think I should just put all this behind me. I mean, what's done is done. Besides, I'm trying to get up out of here anyway."

"What! Come on. I know you ain't trying to let that nigga get away with this bullshit, Twin. The muthafucka left you for dead, and you wanna put that behind you?"

"Princess, I almost died, and that shit scares me. I ain't trying to get caught up in some bullshit with the same muthafucka that tried to kill me. And anyway, what's it to you? You act like you're the one with the vendetta."

"What? I'm trying to look out for you, but if you don't feel like your life is worth getting payback, fuck it then! Have a good night." Princess turned the tables on Twin. Of course, she had her motives, but she couldn't disclose them.

"Yeah, whatever." Twin slammed the car door behind her and headed back to the house. She thought about what Princess said, there were two male voices present the night she was shot, she thought.

Twin sat in the dark, deep in her thoughts. For more than twenty minutes, when suddenly the sounds of Mary J. Blige's song *Not Gon' Cry''* started playing. Twin's eyes started to water as she replayed in her mind over and over again her tragic ordeal.

## Chapter Forty-Eight

Twin had replayed that deadly night over and over again in her head for the last couple of days. It was clear now that Hershey was the one responsible for her being shot.

Because she was so focused on nothing but her newfound recollection, Cadillac Dave's phone calls were the only thing that made her feel better. He would phone her whenever he could, just to let her know she was in his thoughts. Their relationship was quickly growing strong, and he made it clear that he wanted to take things to the next level by asking her to come live with him.

Twin wasted no time giving him her answer. She excitedly blurted out "yes!" Without putting any thought into it. She didn't care whether it was too soon or if it would even work out. Love had nothing to do with it. All she wanted was to leave the hood and to live her life in a rich man's world.

As much as her gut was telling her to move on and put her past behind her, though, she just couldn't until Hershey paid for what he had done to her. After putting as much thought into it as she possibly could, she phoned Princess.

"What's up?" Princess answered, recognizing Twin's number from the caller ID.

"Princess, listen. I've been thinking about what you said and you're right. That son of a bitch has to pay for trying to take my life away."

"So, what, you ready to fuck with K'Dub?" Princess questioned.

"Yeah, if he's the one that could help me."

"Hell yeah, he's the one, plus he got it bad for you, Twin. All you gotta do is get the nigga open, and I'm telling you he'll probably do whatever you want him to."

"But if Hershey is his boy, how am I gonna get him to get at him for me?" Twin asked.

"Come on, Twin. Good pussy can make a nigga do anything. This is me you talking to, and I know you know how to put it down for your crown.  Just manipulate the shit out of his ass and make him think you feeling him like that, then set him up for the kill."

"A'ight, I got you."

"Cool.  I'ma set it up, so expect his call, a'ight?"

"Okay!" Ending the call, Twin felt jitters.  She was a little nervous about the plan.

It has to work, she thought, because nobody fucks over Shamiya Chante Hunt and gets away with it.

## Chapter Forty-Nine

Princess wasted no time getting on it. As soon as she got off the phone with Twin, she phoned K'Dub and made arrangements to meet with him at IHOP for breakfast. He agreed. Princess got up, showered, and dressed. On her way out the door, she glanced over and rolled her eyes, disgusted with Marcus. He was on the couch, where he'd been sleeping for the past couple of nights, since she began her silent treatment.

When she got in her car, she turned on her cell phone and retrieved the six messages that were waiting on her.

Message one: "Yeah, bitch, I see you trying to front on me, huh? A'ight, ho, I'ma see you!"

Message two: "Princess Franklin, how 'bout this, you can ignore my calls all you want, but my people will be seeing you, a'ight!"

Message three, four and five were pretty much the same. Seven went from calling her Princess to her government name and admitted she knew who her man was and where they lived. Now Princess began to fret.

She pulled up to the IHOP, went inside, and was seated. Of course, K'Dub had her waiting for over thirty minutes, and when she arrived, he was freshly dipped in a pair of at least four-carat diamond earrings, a Nike sweatsuit, all white Uptowns, and a platinum link chain with an iced-out Jesus piece on it. Princess never understood how a nigga out to do so much dirt could walk around sporting Jesus on a chain.

Look at this character, she thought, pissed assuming that her money probably paid for all his shit.

"P-Money, what up? What it do, girl?" K'Dub smiled as he slid into the booth next to her.

"What's up? Why you always gotta keep a bitch waiting, huh?"

"Yo, what's up? Oh, wait. Let me order some food first. A nigga starving." K'Dub looked at the menu, disregarding her attitude and her question.

"The two ordered breakfast before Princess began conducting business.

"Listen, I know you heard that the police ran up in the Candy Shop and shut shit down, right?" Princess asked.

"Nah, when this happen?"

Princess knew he was lying, but she didn't call him on it. She just continued on about Seven getting caught up in the sweep.

"A'ight, so why is you telling me?" K'Dub questioned.

"I'm telling you 'cause the bitch is locked the fuck up and she's making threats to snitch me out. Her bail is five g's and I ain't got that, and if I ain't got that, then you know I ain't got the money to keep paying your fucking ass for the bullshit you got me on. Don't you think we've played this game long enough? Me and Marcus, ain't working out, but I'm willing to do you a favor if you could front me the money, for Seven's bail, and after I pay you back, we're even."

K'Dub laughed at her.

"What kind of favor you gon' do for me that's gonna cost me five g's? That shit sounds funnier than a muthafucka!" He said. "Anyway, what's up with your pill connect? The Candy Shop ain't the only strip joint you could sell them shit's at."

"I know that, but my connect ain't fucking with me no more. The last time I went to check him, he told me that that was my last play, 'cause he was giving it up and moving to Chicago," Princess lied. Truth be told, she didn't want to do it anymore, but she knew if she told K'Dub that, his greed would get in the way.

She no longer cared about him telling Marcus about her rendezvous with Lucky. Besides, she knew K'Dub would dig up some more dirt against her, because he was that type of nigga. He's trying to blackmail me, the same way D'Lamar did to Leah. So, fucking what if we let Lucky lick our pussy? It ain't none of his fucking business. I just want all debts to be settled.

"Oh, word. So, if that stripper bitch ain't get knocked, you still would've been ass out, huh?" K'Dub asked.

"Yeah, I guess, but at least I would've had the dough she made for the week. Anyway, that's neither here nor there. Do we got a deal or what?" Princess questioned.

"Yo, I ain't heard no deal. What I'm giving you five g's for, and why you ain't ask my man Marcus?"

"Cause he's the reason I ain't got it! Remember y'all little investment? Don't worry. As soon as I get my cut from him, I give you my word, I'll give it back to you.

"You feeling my home girl Twin, right? I could hook that up for you --you know, wash my back and I'll wash yours."

"Get the fuck out of here." He laughed. "You want me to pay you for that? Yo, she already tried that. And I'ma tell you like I told her: The kid doesn't pay for no pussy. A'ight, yo!"

I'm not asking you to pay for nothing. Are you listening? I said loan! C'mon K'Dub, one good deed deserves another. You been hitting my pockets hard. There's gotta be a reason why you wanted me to hook you and Twin up, so what is it? You already hit it, so why don't you just step to her again?"

"Yo, shit went sour between us, that's all."

Princess ignored his bald-faced lie. "So, when you gon' give me the money?" She continued.

"When you hook that up!"

"Come on, K'Dub. Don't fucking try to play me."

"Yo, I'm not. I'm trying to get at her," K'Dub said.

"Then when you give me the money, I'll call her, so you could do that."

"What, you don't trust me?"

"Princess didn't answer. She just gave him a look that said, nigga, that's an understatement.

"A'ight, a'ight. He got the message. "I'll have it for you later on today. K'Dub got up from the table and left, leaving her stuck with the bill.

Princess just shook her head. What a desperate, thirsty muthafucka.

# Von Diesel

## Chapter Fifty

"My name is Dorothy Smith St. John, honey. I'm Swerve's mother. I know what you're probably thinking right now but give me the chance to explain. There are a few things that you need to know. The first thing is to stay away from Black. He means you no good, and he is a dangerous man."

"Excuse me? Swerve's mother? Swerve told me that you were dead," said Rhapsodee.

"It's a long story. I had to stage my death. Swerve's father was in a lot of trouble with some Haitian's because of greed in the drug game. He was fronted a lot of product and in return, never paid his debt. The Haitian's were going to start taking out his closest family members, so I grabbed my two boys and got the hell outta dodge. I gave one away to my sister, Floretta, and I kept the other one with me, which was James, Swerve he calls himself.

After I staged my death, Swerve was given a few million dollars in insurance money. I left instructions for him to leave town and never come back. Once my husband, Big Earl found out about the amount of money Swerve inherited, he sent his half-brother to find him and bring him back to him so that he could take his money and pay the Haitian's off. I don't wish to be the bearer of bad news, but Black is my stepson, and he's Swerve's half-brother. Baby, Black is a dangerous man, just like his father. I advise you to stay away from him. I later found out that Black and E-Love were the ones who put the hit out on my son while he was in jail. This is how he ended up stabbed in the throat."

"Look lady, I don't know who the fuck you think you talking to, but Swerve's mother is dead, and how dare you talk about Black like he some type of killer or something? You got some fucking nerves."

"I need for you to hear me out. I followed Black and his partner, Sosa, to Yoshi's apartment. I later saw Yoshi jump from the third floor of her apartment building. Black and Sosa emerged trying to get away. Sosa was apprehended by the police and taken away to the jail. Black, on the other hand, chose to have a shootout with them pigs. Some kind of way, he managed to get away.

"What?" Rhapsodee questioned.

"Yoshi's two sons were released to my custody after I explained to Social Services that I was their grandmother. I know this is all too much for you to soak in right now, but those boys look just like my son and there was no way in hell I could allow some white folks to take them away to a group home or something."

"So, you're telling me that Black is Swerve's brother?" asked Rhapsodee.

"Yes, honey, he's his half brother. Black has always been jealous of James and his Twin brother J'Shon."

"Hold up, did you say twin brother?" questioned Rhapsodee.

"Yes, he has a twin. And Black will do anything to destroy the both of them. Promise you'll stay far away from Black until we can figure all of this out."

"I...I promise," said Rhapsodee.

"I need you to meet me at the hospital ASAP. I gotta talk my son out of his coma."

"I'm on my way," said Rhapsodee.

## Chapter Fifty-One

Leah covered her mouth with her hand as her heart raced from uncertainty. She was home alone, but something wasn't right.

Her sixth sense caused the hairs on the back of her fragile neck to stand up, and she froze. Suddenly every sound in her house was amplified, and she listened closely. The sounds of weight shifting against her hard-wood floors sent warning bells off in her head.

Someone is in here, she thought. She remembered plugging her phone up on the charger downstairs, and she began to creep slowly, cautiously out of her room. She had no idea who was in her home, and her first instincts were to run, but when she thought of her twins, she was filled with blind courage. She went into E-Love's closet and pulled out a chrome .45.

Leah had a loaded gun stashed in every room of the house, just in case, and she pulled the chamber just like he'd taught her as she walked timidly out of the room. Her aim was so shaky that the gun was more for show than an actual threat, but she kept creeping through the house, waiting for someone to jump out of the shadows. Every sound was amplified, including her own shallow breaths, as anxiety pulsed through her.

"E baby? Is that you down there?" she called out. She already knew the answer to her question. Her gut told her that something was wrong.

The sound of a dining chair scraping across the floor caused her to jump as her neck whipped toward the direction of her kitchen. Undoubtedly, she was not alone, but running away was not an option--not when her children's lives were at stake.

She swallowed the nervous lump in her throat. There were two people in the house, but as Leah made her way to confront the intruder, she knew that only one of them would be walking out of there alive.

"Fuck!" E-Love mouthed as he bumped into the chair. He knew that Leah had heard the noise. The still house seemed to vibrate from the loud sound. She heard E-Love drawing near, and she knew that she couldn't make it out of the back door without being seen. She wasn't ready for her presence to be known.

Leah looked around frantically, knowing that she didn't have time to make an exit. She cursed beneath her breath as she slid into the full-size kitchen pantry. She adjusted the wooden slats on the door so that she couldn't be seen, and she held her breath as she watched the intruder enter the room.

Leah could hear her own pounding fear as she looked around the kitchen, gun ready, heart uneasy. She had turned on every single light in her home as she moved from room to room. She looked at her dining room set. It was as she had left it--precise, clean, all chairs in the correct position.

I know what I heard, she thought as she lowered the gun while turning around in a full circle, confused. There's nobody here? she thought skeptically. Breathing a sigh of uncertain relief, she put her hand on her forehead, sweeping her messy hair off of her face. She was paranoid and on edge. The entire situation had her discombobulated.

Just as she put her guard down completely, she heard someone walk up behind her. Before she even had time to think logically, she turned around and fired a wild shot.

"Whoa! Ma, it's me, E-Love!" he shouted as he raised his hands defensively and looked at her like she was insane. He looked over his shoulder at the hole she had blown through the wall, knowing that she had barely missed him.

"Oh my God! I'm so sorry. I thought--" Flustered, she tried to explain. "I don't know what I thought. I heard someone in the house and--" She couldn't even get the words out of her mouth before the floodgates let up and tears overflowed.

"It's a'ight, ma. There's nobody here but me. It's okay. Everything is going to be a'ight" he said as he stepped to her, giving her a shoulder to cry on. Let it out."

E-Love wrapped his arms around her shoulders, and she poured all into him. She was so vulnerable that she would accept strength from anyone at that point.

"Baby, what happened to your leg?" What the fuck!"

"Calm down, I was shot last night."

"Shot? By who? Are you okay?" asked Leah.

"Yeah, I checked myself out of the hospital. The less you know right now, the better. Help me to the bedroom."

Von Diesel

## Chapter Fifty-Two

*Ding! Dong!*

Leah opened the door and was greeted by two delivery men.

"Leah Langford?" one of the men asked.

Confused, she replied," uh…yeah, I'm Leah."

"We have a furniture delivery for you," the guy said as he handed her a clipboard. Leah frowned, but gave him her John Hancock and then watched as they carried a $10,000 Italian leather group into her home. She smiled slightly, thinking that it was a gift from E-Love that would lift her spirits, but she was too low to truly appreciate the thoughtfulness.

E-Love came into the room, and without speaking he walked over to the furniture.

"Can you hand me the box cutter from the kitchen drawer?" he asked.

Leah did as she was told and winced when she saw him cut into the leather furniture.

"E-Love, what are you doing?" she asked. But when she saw the plastic-wrapped kilos that he pulled out of the couch, she fully understood.

Leah remained silent as she watched an injured E-Love put the bricks in several duffle bags. The police pulled out of his stash spots. Their attention had been turned elsewhere, and although his and Bobby B's case was still open, they had little help now that it would ever be solved. With D'Lamar dead, E-Love was able to move freely. The last thing he needed was a watchful eye over him while he was trying to move weight.

Red Bean had made good on his promise and had E-Love's package delivered to him.

The night was too still. Everything seemed so peaceful as Leah looked out her second story bedroom window, but a storm was brewing. She could feel it. The red numbers on her alarm clock were a horrible reminder of the lack of sleep she was suffering from. She had only taken catnaps here and there, but true peace of mind had been evasive. She couldn't rest with D'Lamar black mailing her about her little secret affair with Lucky. Paying him hush money was too much to consume. She stayed up day and night as her body begged for a break.

She turned toward the bed where E-Love lay. The bandages on his leg were soaked in blood, and she knew that he needed to be in a hospital, but he refused. He insisted that he remain at home with her. Attempting to be her rock was slowly killing him. His snore was a result of the pain medication rather than true dreams. She tightened her short silk robe and walked over to his bedside.

"I love you," she whispered as she bent over him and kissed his forehead. The night was so still that the sound of feet against her walkway erupted in her ears like a bomb. She didn't know if it was her nerves that put her on edge, but she rushed to the window as a bad omen swept over her.

Her hand flew to her mouth in disbelief as her eyes widened. "E-Love...E-Love!" she screamed. Our babies, our babies...someone is kidnapping our babies."

He jumped up and ran to the window. "What the fuck!"

## Chapter Fifty-Three

K'Dub kept his word. Two hours later after he left her at breakfast, they met up and he had the five G's for Princess.

Surprised that he really came through, Princess was even more shocked that he was going so hard at the chance to fuck with Twin again. If she knew that was what it took to get Seven out of jail and keep his ass off her back, she would've hooked him up a long time ago.

It was time to keep her end of the bargain. She dialed Twin, but after a few rings, her voicemail picked up. Princess ended the call and dialed her again, still ending up with her voicemail.

K'Dub was starting to get a little uptight, thinking Princess was trying to pull a fast one on him.

"Yo, Princess, this is some bullshit. Just forget it, a'ight. Gimme my shit back, yo!"

"Yo, nigga, pump yo brakes. I already told her you are feeling her, so just take her number and holla at her later."

"Nah, fuck that. That wasn't the plan. You supposed to hook that shit up in front of me."

"Well, I can't do shit if she doesn't answer, right?"

"Yo, that's why I'm saying fuck it. Just gimme my loot back."

"Wait. I'ma keep trying until I get her."

"Nah, yo, I ain't got all fucking day!"

"K'Dub, here, just leave a message. I promise she'll call you back," Princess said, passing him her cell phone, while it was ringing Twin's phone.

"Huh, what up, ma? This K'Dub. Holla back, a'ight love." He left his phone number on the message too.

"Now, was that so hard?" Princess asked.

"Nah, but shorty better holla back or else me and you gon' have a serious beef, word up!" K'Dub threatened.

"Trust me, she'll call. Damn, what the fuck she did that got you so strung the fuck out, nigga? Princess was curious because K'Dub was acting a little too desperate and nervous.

"Yo, she ain't do shit," K'Dub answered hostilely.

"Whatever, nigga, just hold on tight to your phone, so you don't miss her call. Oh, and here's her cell number just in case."

"A'ight. Stop talking shit and hurry up and get Seven out 'fore she bust that ass." K'Dub laughed, taking the piece of paper from Princess.

Princess ignored his snide remark, but that's exactly what she was on her way to do--post Seven's bail and be out. As she started up her car and pulled off, she tried dialing Twin again just to see if she'd answer, and this time, she did.

"Hello?"

"Oh, now you answer," Princess said sarcastically.

"Girl, I'm sorry I was on the phone with my boo, and the shit he was talking was sounding too good to be put on hold. But anyway, what's good?" Twin asked.

"Well, damn, I'm glad my life didn't depend on you answering your phone and what's good is the same shit we already talked about, unless your boo got you having a change of heart."

"You know what, Princess? I'm in a good mood, so I'm not even gonna entertain your smart ass, a'ight."

"Yeah, okay. Just check your message and hit that nigga back!" Princess demanded and abruptly ended the call.

Ooooh, I can't stand that bitch. Twin retrieved K'Dub's message and phoned him.

"Yo, who dis?" K'Dub wasn't familiar with the number.

"Who you been expecting?" Twin said in a sensual tone.

"Yo, don't play games. Who this?" K'Dub asked again. Even though he assumed it was Twin, he ain't want to seem like he was beasting.

"Damn, my feelings are hurt. I thought you were waiting on my call."

"C'mon, ma, you know I been waiting to talk to you. What up, though?"

"I don't know. My girl Princess told me that you were checking for me."

"Yeah, you don't remember me?" K'Dub questioned.

"From where?"

148

"I don't know, around, I guess. But yo, that's neither here nor there. I'm trying to see you, ma."

"Not a problem."

"Cool. I'ma call you later at this number when I'm ready to scoop you, a'ight."

"No doubt. See you then!"

Von Diesel

## Chapter Fifty-Four

All Princess did was post Seven's bail. She didn't care how the girl got home, or if she even had money to get home. As far as she was concerned, her part was done.

Princess was actually relieved now that she felt she and K'Dub had resolved their issues, and once she paid him back, she would no longer be debt to him. The Lucky drama was dead, and with Seven bailed out, all the skeletons in her closet were gone.

"Yo, Princess, this bullshit gotta stop between us," Marcus said as soon as she walked in the apartment.

"Stop what, Marcus? Your lying or your cheating?"

"Come on, baby, how long you trying to be mad at a nigga?"

"Marcus, you know what? Right now, you better be glad all I'm doing is giving you the silent treatment, 'cause I could go out and get me a nigga that knows how to treat a bitch. Instead, I stay stuck like glue to your muthafucking ass, and what do you do? Nothing but talk shit, lie, and bring fucking diseases home."

"Disease? Yo, what you mean disease? Ain't nothing wrong with my dick." Since Marcus had no symptoms, he had no ideas what she was talking about.

"Oh, nigga, you ain't go get your dick checked yet? That's right, disease, muthafucka. You know, the shit you get when you out in them streets fucking nasty hoes with no condom," Princess sarcastically yelled.

"Yo, I don't know what you are talking about. I suppose I gave you something. What I give you, huh?" Marcus didn't have a clue.

"Nigga, you gave me Chlamydia from being out there with other bitches. Play stupid if you want to, but you better hope my other tests come back negative."

"Yo, I ain't never heard of that, but if I did, I'm sorry. I ain't fucked around on you in a minute, though. Sometimes, I think something's wrong with me, like maybe I got the same shit that Swerve got. I don't know why I be fucking other bitches. I just do. I'ma go get my shit checked out, so you can stop being mad at me, please."

Marcus always had a way with words and as much as Princess didn't want to fall victim to his bullshit, she couldn't help it. She suffered from a sickness called love. She just loved him. She didn't know why, but she did. He was always able to break her down, and love was stronger than pride. Princess forgave him, but only on one condition: Her tests had to come back negative.

## Chapter Fifty-Five

On his way to meet up with Twin, K'Dub couldn't help but feel a little nervous about fucking with her again, especially the way he dogged her the first time. It was like she had some kind of hex on him, but he still felt sort of obsessed over her. Honestly, he regretted forcing himself on her and wanted another chance with her.

Twin wasn't comfortable with K'Dub picking her up from her apartment, so she arranged for him to meet her at this cozy little restaurant on Panola Road. She waited for him to arrive, so they could go in and be seated together.

The dimly lit restaurant was small but always packed. The tables were so close together that it almost felt like people were sitting on top of each other, but for some reason, no one seemed to mind.

There was a long period of silence between the two. Twin stared at K'Dub often. Her intent looks made him a little apprehensive, but she couldn't help it, because something about him seemed all too familiar.

"I'm sorry I keep looking at you so hard, but there's something about you--I just don't know what it is," Twin said, breaking the silence first.

"Stop trying to figure it out and let's just have a good time. We could start by ordering some drinks." Rudely, he flagged down the waiter. Twin ordered an apple martini, and since K'Dub was feeling the guilt eat away at him, he ordered a Grey Goose mixed with Hennessy and a splash of cranberry juice to help mellow him out.

The alcohol did ease the tension a bit, as the two began to converse a little more. K'Dub complimented everything from Twin's hairstyle to her shoes and also ran a few dry jokes by her. Twin chilled on the hard looks and pretended to find his jokes funny.

After dinner, K'Dub wasn't ready to call it a night just yet, so he suggested that she follow him to this little bar on Klondike called Deja Vu. All Twin could think about was getting home in time for her midnight call from Cadillac Dave. She tried to refuse but ended up giving in to his pleas and agreed to go and have one drink.

When they walked inside the bar, they both stopped to check out the pictures posted up on the wall from the previous parties held there. From the looks of it, everybody seemed to be having a great time.

As they took a seat at the bar, Twin glanced around to check out the spot. She could tell it had a nice vibe to it, and since the crowd looked to be a mature one, there wasn't a lot of rowdiness. The bartender, Von, was very friendly as she took their drink orders, and K'Dub went on to boast to Twin about a popular book the bartender wrote entitled *"Hard and Ruthless"*. Twin didn't find that to be all that impressive, but she did like the way the girl made her apple martini strong.

*"Hard and Ruthless?"* Sounds pretty interesting. I remember wanting to be an author. I wrote several books in the past, but never sent them off to a publisher. Is she an urban author?"

"Yeah, I think *"Hard and Ruthless,"* was her first book. Shid, that was like the first book I actually picked up. A nigga can't wait to buy part two of that shit, it gives me something to look forward to," said K'Dub.

"Maybe I can send my manuscript to her publisher. What's the name of the book again, I wanna look it up online and see who the publisher is?" asked Twin.

*"Hard and Ruthless,"* K'Dub replied. "Part one of the trilogy is *"Hard and Ruthless(Taste My Gangsta)*, and part two is called *"Hard and Ruthless(Test My Gangsta)."*

"Oh snap, she writes for that nigga Ca$h, yeah…I gotta get in on this. He might just be interested. Nothing beats a try."

One drink ended up turning into three as they both started to unwind around each other. Twin had to admit that his jokes got better, and so did her liking for him (after the alcohol kicked in, of course). K'Dub was doing his best to keep her entertained, hoping that his jokes mixed with the strong-ass drinks would land him up in the pussy again, only this time not by force. Unfortunately for him, that thought was more of a pipe dream, 'cause yeah, he might have been given a second crack at her, but the game was still the same as far as Twin was concerned. Her goodies stayed in the jar until a nice amount of money had been spent. It was gonna cost him a little more than a meal and some drinks to taste her cookie.

As soon as 11:30 hit, Twin decided to call it a night. Leaning over, she planted a soft kiss on his lips.

"Good night."

Damn, he thought, caught a little off guard as the softness of her lips and the whiff of her scent made his dick rise.

"You leaving me already?" K'Dub questioned with disappointment.

"Yeah, I have to go. I finally recognize where I know you from though," Twin said.

"What?" Twin responded tensely as his heart began to pound.

"Yeah, I remember you now, from Curtis Place a while back. You were at the bar with Marcus and some other guy."

"Oh, yeah. Okay, right, right!" K'Dub answered as he let out a deep sigh of relief. He didn't know how he was gonna fuck with Twin without the torture of worrying about when, or if, she would ever remember how much she really hated him and why.

As Twin left, K'Dub waited for a few moments and then secretly followed her to her home for the hell of it.

Von Diesel

## Chapter Fifty-Six

A couple weeks passed, and things were all good between Princess and Marcus, especially since her test results came back negative. She even escorted him to the clinic to get tested. Since Marcus knew he was running around fucking everything in sight, he took it a step further and agreed to be tested for HIV. Princess still refused to take an HIV test, because she felt that since his results came back negative, then she was negative, and HIV was as simple as that.

Princess was also able to relax more without the static from Seven. Maybe Seven wasn't upset about having to stay in jail a couple of days and was just happy to be home, so she decided to let it go. Marcus and K'Dub were still handling their business, and money would soon be straight for them.

Now K'Dub was all caught up in Twin, therefore Marcus and his friendship turned into more of just a business partnership. Of course, Princess was happy about that, because that meant Marcus, ran the streets less and spent more time with her. They were finally starting to connect. They laid up for the most the day watching movies, making love, getting high, and even talking about one day having kids. It all seemed too good to be true, because in the three years that she'd been with him, all they ever seemed to do was fight, fuss and fuck. Sure, he claimed to love her, but this was the first time since his bid that she actually felt his love for her.

She felt the time was right to clear her conscience and pull all her skeletons out of the closet. She told him that she was bi-sexual and about her brief relationship with Lucky. To her surprise, Marcus already knew. He said he had gotten the word months ago.

"How?" Princess questioned, anxious to know the answer and hoping it wasn't K'Dub that told.

"Yo, don't worry about it. Just know I know!"

"Well, were you mad when you heard?"

"What, I'ma be mad for? Baby girl, you be holding a nigga down, so how I'ma knock your hustle? The shit about you fucking with that bitch, man, I knew as soon as daddy came back home, that shit was gon' be a wrap!" Marcus said.

For the first time in a long time, Princess was able to exhale. She was glad to know that she didn't have to stress over none of her secrets anymore, but she also knew K'Dub put a twenty-thousand-dollar dent in her pocket for nothing.

Marcus caught Princess gazing off into a deep thought.

"Yo, is there something else you gotta tell me?"

"Nah, that's it," Princess smiled and snapped out of her trance.

"A'ight then, climb up on daddy's dick and give me some of that pussy," Marcus ordered.

Princess was more than happy to obey his order. Just as she was about to lay it down, there was a hard knock at the door.

"Who the fuck is that knocking like they crazy?" Oh, boy, I bet it's K'Dub's stupid ass," Princess said, slightly raising her voice as if her high was just blown. She got up out of bed and threw on something to go see.

Swinging open the door, expecting to see K'Dub, she was surprised to find four policemen standing there. Her heart dropped. She knew it would be only a matter of time before she was busted.

"Princess Monique Franklin, you're under arrest for the intent to sell and distribute drugs. You have the right to remain silent..." The arresting officer read her rights, handcuffed her and hauled her off to jail.

## Chapter Fifty-Seven

Marcus rushed down to the precinct to see what was up with Princess. The arresting officers wouldn't disclose any information other than that she was being brought up on felony charges. He took that little bit of info for what it was worth and immediately called his lawyer, Mr. Dean, to explain the situation and ask if he'd take her case. His attorney agreed.

Marcus continued calling Princess's mom, Ms. Diane, but she hated him and would definitely use this situation as an opportunity to badger him. That was the last thing he needed right now, especially since he had nothing to do with this mess Princess had gotten herself into. The only thing left for him to do was go home and wait for Princess to call him.

After hours of interrogation, name calling and harsh threats, Princess managed to hold her head. She wasn't confessing nothing. The police had some solid evidence against her. Not only did Seven drop dime, but her supplier's perverted ways finally caught up with him, and he sang like a bird when the feds nabbed him. Apparently, an underage girl accused him of drugging her and then trying to have his way with her. Seven, also told the police that he was a big-time drug dealer, which they already suspected.

Princess was not only concerned about her ties with her supplier, but the police confiscated several security tapes from his house, some with her on them. Still, Princess refused to talk. The only words she had for them were: "Can I make my phone call. Now?"

Von Diesel

## Chapter Fifty-Eight

"Free at last, Free at last! Thank God Almighty, I'm free at last!" I loudly recited the famous words of Dr. Martin Luther King, Jr. As I exited the confines of Fulton County Jail.

After spending four days there, a nigga was happy to get out. When I was originally booked on the lesser assault charge after speaking with the detectives, I went to speak with the magistrate about a bond. That bitch as nigga denied me bail, claiming that I was a flight risk, since I was actually from out of state, so I had to wait to get another bond hearing. When I went before another judge, he granted me a $30,000 bond. I got in touch with a bondsman, and he let me out for two grand.

I waited patiently for my cab to arrive and literally jumped for joy when I saw him pull up.

"Yippee!" I skipped to the cab like a little kid and hopped in the back seat. The Westin Hotel downtown." I directed him to the hotel, because I would be there hiding out for a couple of days.

As soon as the cabby pulled up, I got myself a room and then walked around to West End Terminal, where my car originally had been parked.

I made my way to the interstate and headed towards Columbus, to my parent's crib to pick up my lil' shawty. I'd gotten my own little pad in Atlanta, but I rarely spent any time there.

As I was driving, the scene from Yoshi's apartment was playing over and over in my head. The two things most disturbing to me were, one, I'd witnessed Black almost shoot the shit out of Yoshi's son, and two, I was so damn close to death myself. I knew in my heart that Black would not have hesitated to put a bullet in me just as fast if he knew what I was about to do. With that in mind, I began to reflect back on the agreement I'd made with Detective Willis. What the fuck have I done? I wondered to myself, realizing I had made a big mistake. I've just given myself a death sentence. Black is gonna fucking kill me. I'm never gonna make it to court.

My brain started racing, and my nerves were starting to get the best of me. If Black found out, I was an eyewitness, and planned to testify against him, he would make sure I didn't have breath left in my body. As paranoia set in, I began constantly looking in my side-view and rear-view mirrors to see if someone was following me. I was beginning to feel like a fucking lunatic fleeing from the crazy house.

For a moment, I could have sworn that a black, tinted-out Tahoe was following me. I was so shook. My tank was empty, but I refused to get gas. When I finally was forced, I circled the gas station two times to be sure no one was following me into the station. I pumped my gas and jumped back on the interstate in record breaking time.

As I continued to drive, my brain was constantly plagued by this whole Black situation, so I decided to give Detective Willis a call.

"Willis," he answered on the first ring.

"Yo, man, this Sosa. I just worked out a deal with you involving the murder at Lakeview Apartments."

"What's up, Sosa? What can I do for you?"

"Well, I was wondering if Black would be informed that I will be testifying, because I'm a little worried about my safety."

"Well, we will inform him there is an eyewitness, but we won't reveal who until the court proceeding. But you don't have to worry. Once we get our hands on him, he will not be coming out, and until then, you need to lay low and we will do all we can to make sure you're protected. Don't you worry."

"Okay," I said, still not feeling anymore confident that I'd felt before the call. Actually, I felt worse.

I knew, after talking to the Detective, there was no way I could go through with the deal we negotiated. These days it was easier to beat the system than the streets. I could buck on court and be on the run and live to talk about it, as opposed to testifying against Black and not even making it to court.

Now that I'd made my mind up that I wasn't going to court to testify against Black not my charge for that matter, I had to put an escape plan into play. I knew it was nothing to relocate. I could easily go someplace like Trinidad and live with no problem. I knew a few people there. Plus, I would be in heaven, with so much Trinidadian pussy to choose from.

The only downfall would be leaving my family, baby momma, and worst of all, my five-year-old son, who I would give my life for. I'm sure I could probably live without my sorry ass drug addicted, gone-bad, baby momma, Ranequa. Hell, she was part of the reason I had to resort to the streets. The thought of being away from my kid was killing me. Deep inside, I knew it would be too risky to have him with me while I was on the run.

# Von Diesel

## Chapter Fifty-Nine

As he walked down what appeared to be a very long tunnel, Swerve heard a voice calling his name. It was coming from behind him. The voice was a female and it sounded familiar. Afraid, she paused for a moment as the voice continued to call out his name. It was as if she had something important to say.

Swerve hesitantly turned around. Something inside of him forced him to follow the voice. As he followed the voice, he could see a beaming ray of light, and the further he walked, the brighter the light got. The light was his guide. Suddenly, he could see images of his life posted up on the tunnel's walls. The good, the bad, and the ugly had all been caught on film. He felt like he was trapped in a projection room that featured the life and times of James St. John.

There were moments he'd spent as a child with his parents, moments with friends, and X-rated moments he'd shared with many women.

This is some weird shit, Swerve thought, but being vain, he found this experience to be fascinating, watching his life, his memories, and his personal moments. All of it, from adolescence to adulthood, surrounded him. This was either his journey to heaven or hell, the weighing of his good deeds and his sins.

As he continued down the long tunnel, the sound of his name became louder. When he finally reached the end, he saw Rhapsodee smiling at him. She was butt-ass naked, with a satin red bow tied around her. She looked like a gift from heaven. He had been calling out to her all along.

Once he approached her, no words were exchanged, and although she was smiling, he could see that there was some sadness in her eyes. He wrapped his arm around her tightly, as if he would never see her again. Her body temperature was so cold. Swerve tried to speak to her, but his words could not escape his mouth. He felt numb.

Suddenly, darkness filled the hall. Everything had faded right before his eyes--Rhapsodee, the images, and the light. Swerve stood alone at the end of the tunnel. Rhapsodee had just saved him from eternal darkness and it was time for him to go home.

Swerve's mom noticed slight movement from Swerve for the first time. His eyelids were shut, but his eyeballs moved as if he was trying to open them.

"It's been five weeks. Wake up and come out of that misery," his mom whispered as she reached for her son's hand. "I know you're a fighter. Your wife knows you're a fighter, and even these doctors know, baby. Make your way back. You're too strong to be lying up in this damn hospital bed like this. Do you hear me?"

Swerve didn't respond with words, but he squeezed his mother's hand just enough to let her know he heard her. That was all the assurance Momma D needed. She knew that Swerve would pull through for sure now.

Momma D definitely wanted Black and E-Love to suffer as well, but just not at the hands of her husband. She faked her death so that Big Earl would give up that gangsta shit, and there was no way she was going back to living that kind of lifestyle with him. Taking care of Black and E-Love was something she had to do.

Swerve had been lying in a coma for five weeks, but let Momma D tell it, it seemed like months or years, and every day was a struggle. Momma D looked toward the Lord to pull her through.

She had always believed in him, although she never appreciated how good he'd been to her and her family over the years. It took a tragedy to open her eyes and make her realize that she had a lot to be grateful for. Big Earl had been in the drug game for over twenty-five years and somehow, he had never been locked up, shot, robbed or killed.

The only harm that crossed their paths was when Haitian Jack put a hit out on her and her twin boys. Because Big Earl failed to deliver them two million dollars for the drugs that they fronted him. I had no other choice but to give one of the twins to my sister, Floretta. I couldn't care for the both of them while on the run. I later staged my own death, so that Swerve could move on and move freely. My instructions in my will were for Swerve to move as far down south as he possibly could and to never look back.

She was ready to give thanks and praise to the Lord. God only knows, it's long overdue, but never too late. Dorothy Smith St. John joined the born-again Baptist community church, and the changes within her had been miraculous.

"Momma," Swerve said, looking around the hospital room.

Momma D froze in disbelief. The word sounded like a sweet melody, music to her ears.

"Praise the Lord, thank you Jesus," Momma D closed her eyes and said a little prayer. Before rushing to Swerve's bedside.

Right away, Swerve started to panic as he looked around at his unfamiliar surroundings. He began to forcefully pull at the IV tubes in his arms.

Von Diesel

## Chapter Sixty

Twin was spending a lot of time with K'Dub. If she was still interested in niggas making small-time figures, he could've actually won her heart. He accommodated her need to be spoiled, but she wasn't trying to get caught up with him and lose focus on the plan. He was friends with the nigga that tried to kill her, and more than likely, he knew about it.

Twin didn't know what it would take to persuade to kill Hershey for her, but she decided it was time to let K'Dub sample her goodies when she overheard a discussion he was having with Marcus, concerning some conflict with Hershey. She knew he was ready to sever ties with him. Their beef would be the beginning of Hershey's end.

K'Dub started to develop strong feelings for Twin; however, he was growing impatient and tired of doing all the whining, dining, and spending for nothing. He never was that type of nigga to kick out cash for ass, but he was splurging like crazy, and even though he had already hit it once, he was thirsty to find out what it tasted like.

Damn, I guess you should never say never. But fuck it. I'm just gonna throw it out there and ask for some. K'Dub picked up the phone and called to confirm their date.

"Hey, boo." Twin answered.

"What up, ma? We still on for the night?

"Oh, no question. Why? Where you want me to meet you at this time?"

"Yo, why you always gotta meet me? Why can't I just come pick you up?"

"Because."

"Because what? You don't trust me?"

"K'Dub, it ain't about that. You know what happened. I just don't want to bring no bullshit where I lay my head."

"Yeah, a'ight, yo. I guess, I gotta respect that. So meet me at the Marriott at nine o'clock, a'ight."

"Ooooh, so does that mean I should bring something sexy to wear?" Twin said, giving him all the assurance, he needed.

Before he could respond, her other line beeped. It was Cadillac Dave. She rushed off. "Nine o'clock is good. I gotta take this call. Bye." Twin switched over to Cadillac Dave.

"Damn, I miss you, baby," she said seductively.

"For real? I miss you too. I miss you so much I followed you today." Twin's heart pounded rapidly.

"S-stop playing, baby!" she stuttered.

"Yeah, I'm playing, but you saving that stuff for me, right?"

"Oh, no doubt, daddy. This pussy belongs to only you. When you coming for it?" she teased.

"As a matter of fact, I'ma be back in town tomorrow afternoon. So, what's up?" You packing your bags or what?"

"Hell yeah. I can't wait."

"A'ight, sweet sugar panties, I'll pick you up soon as I touch down around noon."

"Okay, baby, as soon as you touch down." Twin repeated.

"I got you," said Cadillac Dave as he hung up the phone.

## Chapter Sixty-One

"Nine-one-one. What is your emergency?"

"Someone took my children. My twins have been kidnapped," Leah whispered with a stifled cry as she covered her mouth to contain her fear.

She turned around and saw E-Love standing in the doorway. She jumped and released the phone as if it had suddenly grown hot in her hand.

"What did you do ma?" he asked as he shook his head from side to side. "Did you forget that I have a shit load of drugs in here? You gotta help me get this shit out of here. Quick, help me put this shit in the truck, I'ma park it in the back of the next-door neighbor's yard, they gone out of town. He knew the magnitude of her actions. Within the hour, their home would be swarming with cops, every part of their lives monitored and picked apart. They were about to be under a federal microscope, and to a hustler of E-Love's stature, that was worse than death. "What did you do?"

Leah looked him directly in the eyes and wiped her tears as she replied, "I did what I had to do...for our kids."

The red, white and blue flashing lights lit up the streets like it was the Fourth of July. While Leah felt a sense of relief from the presence of authority, E-Love's chest tightened uncomfortably. He was cut from a completely different cloth than Leah. Under no circumstances did he trust the police, even something as daunting as the twin's disappearance didn't spark an urge for him to request their help.

Tension thickened the air as Leah looked at E-Love from across the room. She could see his anger in his pulsing temples as he spoke with the lead federal agent in charge of the twin's case. She herself had been questioned a million times in a million different ways. They asked the same questions repetitively in an attempt to find a loophole in her story, but Leah had nothing to hide. She was as honest as she could be, but as she watched E-Love's demeanor, she knew that things were not going as smoothly for him.

Leah could see that E-Love needed her by his side. She was his regulator and could calm him down just by standing beside him. She made her way to him and interrupted the line of questioning that the agent was taking him through.

"Hi. I'm Leah Langford, the twin's mother," she said as she extended one hand and rubbed E-Love's back generously with the other. She could feel his shoulders relaxing from her touch.

"Federal Agent Peterson," he replied as he shook her hand. His tone of voice was tight and unfriendly, his eyes accusatory and stern. Leah could tell that the man would not extend them the benefit of the doubt. He cleared his throat and continued with his interrogation.

"Where were the two of you when your children were taken?" he asked.

"Asleep in the master bedroom," E-Love replied.

"There was no sign of forced entry? Neither of you heard anything. Infants usually cry when their rest is disturbed. You must be a pretty heavy sleeper, huh?"

Leah could hear the sarcasm in his voice, and she frowned slightly, but kept her cool. Now was not the time for theatrics. She didn't care how much of a jerk the guy was, as long as he did his job and recovered her children.

"We don't know how they got in, and we didn't hear anything," E-Love said.

"Hmm, convenient," the agent scoffed.

"Excuse me?" Leah asked.

Peterson shook his head and replied, "That's hard to believe."

Leah was at a loss for words. She didn't know how to respond. The innuendo of guilt that Agent Peterson expressed was enough to let Leah know that she had no ally in him.

Before they could even answer him, he continued, "Do you see how this looks from where I'm sitting? So, tell me what happened. Mrs. Langford, did you accidentally bring harm to your baby? And did dad help you cover your tracks?"

"I would never--" Leah began to defend herself, but Agent Peterson held up a hand to stop her mid-sentence.

"That's what they all say. I've been doing this for a long time, and nine times out of ten, the parents are the guilty party," he stated firmly.

"That's enough," E-Love finally spoke up. "I thought this was an interview, not an interrogation. You can contact my attorney if these are the types of questions you're going to ask. Somebody has my kids, and it would be in your best interest to start doing your job instead of insulting my family."

Peterson smirked, unimpressed and unthreatened by E-Love's show of manhood! "We're going to set up in the living room for forty-eight hours. This could be a ransom kidnapping. All we can do is sit back and wait for the perpetrator to make contact." He began to walk away. His cocky attitude displayed dominance, as if he owned the place.

He stopped when he was halfway across the room and snapped his fingers. "Oh, yeah, Mr. Langford, what line of business did you say you were in?" he asked.

Agent Peterson looked around the plush two-story home while nodding his head in approval. "Whatever it is, must be lucrative," he commented sarcastically as he took in the luxury around him.

E-Love's jaw tightened as he watched local and federal cops take over his home. "This is just the beginning," he said loud enough for only Leah to hear him. "Be careful what you say to them, Leah. If it's not about the twins, they don't need to know," he warned as he kissed her cheek before making his way out of the room.

"E-Love," Leah called to him, but he ignored her calls as he stormed out of the room. E-Love made his way into their master bath and locked the door behind him. There was only so much one man could take. All control had been shifted out of his hands, and the possibility of the twin's safe return was fading. The realization that he may never see them again tore his heart out of his chest. His resolve broke, and as he stared at himself in the mirror, he sobbed silently. It was a moment that he would never share with another soul, tears that were only meant for God to see.

Von Diesel

## Chapter Sixty-Two

Twin arrived at the Marriott at 10:05 p.m. She pulled into a vacant parking spot and took a couple of minutes to apply a little more gloss to her already shiny lips in her rearview mirror. Before getting out of the car, she clutched down on the bottom of her Marc Jacobs bag to make sure she had her .22. She made it a priority to never leave the house without it after her near-death experience. Normally, she would have had her nine, but it never turned up after that night. For her, having some protection was better than none at all. She would say, "A .22 might not kill a muthafucka, but it will definitely complicate their intentions to harm me.

Covering all areas, she was ready for whatever and had her game face on as she pranced toward the hotel entrance, where she found K'Dub waiting inside their room. Twin wasted no time getting down to business. Opening her little overnight bag, she pulled out something more appropriate for the occasion. She suggested K'Dub order a bottle of champagne from room service while she showered and slipped into something sexy for him.

K'Dub liked the idea of her slipping into something sexy. The hood rats he used to fuck with considered a matching bra and panties something sexy, if he was lucky.

The champagne arrived just before Twin opened the steamy bathroom door. She was smelling so fresh and so clean, like cucumber melon, in her red lace Victoria Secret lingerie number. K'Dub was mesmerized. As he held two glasses of bubbly, the bulge in his boxers was starting to show, and he wondered if she tasted as good as she smelled.

Seductively, she walked over to him, removed both glasses from his hands, and one by one took both of them straight to the head. Twin placed the empty glasses down, pushed him onto the bed, and slowly climbed on top of him, gliding her tongue across his chest.

K'Dub's eagerness wouldn't allow him to just lie there and enjoy her foreplay. He wanted Twin--now. Flipping her over, he ripped her panties off and aggressively started licking her pussy.

Twin squirmed from discomfort as he licked and sucked on her with such brute force. She tried to move his head from between her legs, only K'Dub continued like some kind of wild beast in a trance, pinning her legs down to the bed and ignoring her screams for him to stop.

His behavior struck a chord. Suddenly, Twin flashed back to why she hated him in the first place. She remembered him raping her. In a panic, she began to gasp for air. Hysterical, she punched him repeatedly, finally getting him to stop.

She jumped up from the bed, grabbed her purse, and ran in the bathroom. Locking the door behind her, she quickly dumped out her bag, searching for her asthma pump. Calming down after a few minutes, she sat on the bathroom floor, holding her gun in her hand.

Meanwhile, K'Dub stood on the other side of the door, begging for her forgiveness.

"I'm sorry, baby. I don't know what got into me. Please give me another chance. I really care about you, Twin. Come out. We'll just lay down. No sex, I promise."

It was too late. Twin wanted to shoot him through the door, but as badly as she wanted to kill him, she knew she had to see Hershey suffer first. She put her gun away, pushed her feelings to the side, opened the door, and lay in K'Dub's arms, awake for the rest of the night.

In the back of her mind, she smiled and said to herself, "I've got plans for you too nigga."

## Chapter Sixty-Three

Leah watched nervously as every national news station in the country littered her front lawn. The twin's case miraculously made the headlines all over. Out of all the missing kids out there, somehow theirs was interesting enough to make the cut. Their faces were amongst all the white news stories. Nancy Grace, MSNBC Fox, and every local station were all waiting anxiously to witness the reaction of the twin's parents. They were all waiting to either support or persecute Eric and Leah Langford.

Leah stood on the podium in front of her home as she looked out on the flashing lights in front of her. There were so many microphones shoved in her face and cameras aimed directly at her that they made her shake nervously. Her eyes watered as intense pressure of the moment stifled her. The statement that she was about to make would be broadcasted live all over the state of Georgia.

She looked over to E-Love for support, and he nodded his head confidently. The subtle wink that he gave her sent a wave of reassurance over her, and finally she found her voice to speak.

"My name is Leah Langford. Two days ago, my twins were taken from my home in the middle of the night. They are not even one years old yet. They need to be with their family… with me and my husband. Please do not hurt our children. We will do anything for their safe return. They are all we have. This is a mother's plea. To the person responsible for taking them, I beg of you, please just return them to me unharmed."

The look of worry on her face could not be faked by the best of actresses. Leah was distraught, and as the media and the police watched her step down from the podium, they all felt a little bit of her pain. It was as if she had chipped off a tiny piece of it and placed it in their hands.

It was then that the detective concluded that Leah was not a part of this escapade, but as he looked at E-Love, he wasn't so sure. He could smell a drug dealer from a mile away, E-Love fit the bill. The arrogance and shrewd authority that E-Love possessed was a dead giveaway. He was a hustler, and his swagger was too great to conceal. He was too large, and despite the fact that his operation ran with efficiency, he still drew attention.

As Leah stepped off of the platform, she walked directly into E-Love's warm embrace. Although there were people all around him, when her head hit his chest, everyone else disappeared. She closed her eyes and exhaled as he rocked her gently from side to side.

"You did good, ma. Everything will be okay," he said. The more he said it, the better it made her feel, but inside, he was well aware that this thing could end badly.

She looked up at him and frowned. Her heartbeat quickened, but everything else seemed to move in slow motion as she noticed the red dot appear in the middle of his chest. She stepped back from him instinctively and fixed her mouth to warn him, but before the words should even leave her mouth, the red dot disappeared. She then screamed as loud as she could.

The detective rushed over to E-Love and Leah, immediately calling for assistance as he looked around simultaneously for the aimer. He was already suspicious of E-Love's profession, but this confirmed things.

Legit businessmen don't take attempted shots in broad daylight. E-Love ran Atlanta, and although he hid his thuggish nature extremely well, the streets had given him away. Beef was left stinking at his front door, and the detective was about to come sniffing.

## Chapter Sixty-Four

E-Love and Bobby rode through the hood. Black gloves and black masks disguised their identities as they neared their intended destination. No words needed to be exchanged. Everyone had a position to play, and on this cold, Black Saturday, it was time to put in work. The way that they moved, every action had a reaction.

The consequences for snatching the twins would be deadly for anyone involved. The gray overcast sky should have been every indication that it was about to rain, but what Atlanta had never seen before was the downpour that E-Love was about to bring. He wasn't into making it rain dollars... that was for trick niggas, and E-love was about to make it rain bullets, and anyone he ever had beef with was in his crosshairs. The way he felt, the entire fucking city could get it if need be. No one was exempt, and niggas would bleed until he received the answers that he sought, or until his twins returned home safely.

He was highly offended by the trespass that had been committed against him. And as he rode in the backseat of Bobby B's old school '64 Impala, anger consumed him. He was silent, stoic, still. He wasn't a rah-rah type of nigga that talked big. He acted big.

These niggas think it's a stage play. I live this, I do this. I don't play gangsta. I'ma burn this bitch to the ground if something happens to my kids. His brow furrowed deep from a combination of worry and madness. On the outside, one would never know his troubles, but on the inside, there was a bitter and brutal storm brewing. His entire life was flashing before his eyes.

Everything depended on his twin's safe return. He knew that Leah would never get over her grief. If this ended badly, and he would never forgive himself as well.

He was jarred from his thoughts, when the car stopped moving. He stared out of his window.

"You sure you want to do this?" Bobby B asked as he peered intently at E-Love through his rearview mirror.

E-Love didn't even look his way. He simply stared out of the window and nodded his head.

*CLICK-CLACK!*

The sound of E-Love clocking his .380 handgun was the beginning of the end. E-Love was the conductor of this street symphony and he was about to serenade a couple niggas right to sleep.

*BOOM!*

Bobby B had just played the first note. E-Love watched as Bobby B got out of the car and unloaded his semi-automatic pistol on the trap house. They wanted to leave a blood bath behind, sending a message to whoever was in charge. E-Love knew it had something to do with pain that he inflicted upon D'Lamar and that these were the niggas bringing the heat to his front door.

He was a man, so he stood behind everything that he had ever done but drawing his family into things had been a low blow. A deadly line had been crossed. He showed no mercy when his borders were penetrated. His wife and kids were off limits.

## Chapter Sixty-Five

Twin thought about what happened between her and K'Dub the entire night. Allowing herself to be in his company again sickened her. She didn't feel comfortable playing this little game anymore. All types of thoughts started to cross her mind, mainly that maybe she was the one being played.

K'Dub almost raped me a second time last night and Hershey tried to kill me. Shit, maybe they're scheming to finish me off.

Finally, thinking sensibly, Twin felt seeking revenge this way didn't seem so sweet or safe for her anymore, and it certainly wasn't worth losing her life over (for real this time).

She eased K'Dub's arm from around her, got out of bed and quietly put on her clothes. Before sneaking out, Twin gathered up all K'Dub's belongings, including his cell phone, and took them with her. Inside her car, she emptied out his pockets: $180 in crumpled twenties, a Cartier watch, platinum chain with a diamond-studded Jesus head medallion, a wallet with nine crisp $100 bills, and his license.

Twin started up her car and pulled off. Reaching halfway home, she smiled to herself, thinking, Payback is a bitch.

She stopped at a gas station and tossed the useless possessions--his clothes, sneakers, empty wallet, and phone--in a dumpster. Crying silently to herself. She didn't know if her life was even worth living anymore. Being raped. Damn near shot to death and still alive to tell about it, most people never got the chance.

Paying Hershey and K'Dub back was a must and she wasn't going to stop until she accomplished just that.

She cranked up her car and got back on the interstate. She pulled out her phone and dialed Cadillac Dave's number.

"Yo, what up, shawty, where you at?" Cadillac Dave inquired.

"I'm on my way home baby."

"So, you gon' pack up your shit and head on over or what?" asked Cadillac Dave.

"You want me to pack up everything?" inquired Twin.

"Only if you're promising me a lifetime of forever," explained Cadillac Dave.

"You know I am, baby. I'll be there shortly," Twin said and hung up.

## Chapter Sixty-Six

Princess cried the whole ride over to central booking. She couldn't believe Seven had actually played her like that.

She felt like such an idiot for letting her guard down and befriending Seven. She told her personal things about her and Marcus's sex life, his dick size, how he was always away from home, and even about her alter ego "TEMPTATION", that she used in the dirty online chat rooms. She had to admit she had set herself up for the kill, played right into Seven's hands. She had agreed to inviting strippers that night, when in her heart she was dead set against the whole idea.

By the time Princess finished getting processed it was too late to stand before the judge. Although it was late, she decided to use her one phone call to call Ms. Diane, she was certain she'd reach her. She explained her situation to Ms. Diane and told her that she wouldn't know anything further regarding her release until the morning, which meant she had to spend the night in the bullpen.

Princess had never experienced such filth in her life, locked up with the prostitutes, drug addicts, boosters, and God only knew what else. It was a tight squeeze in the overcrowded cell. With one dingy stall in the corner, the men in the other cell directly across could see everything. The idea of having to stay in a place like this turned her stomach. There was one long wooden bench up against the wall that was so full, women were stretched out in the remaining three corners and all over the floor. With no place to rest, she thought she'd be standing in that one spot for the remainder of the night.

"Here, honey, Come sit next to Big Sexy," a woman said, putting a small space next to her on the bench. Detecting Princesses hesitation, she continued, "Come, honey, I ain't gon' bite you. Shit, I got daughters your age."

"Thanks," Princess said, sitting down.

"No problem, honey. What you in here for?" Big Sexy asked.

"Ahhh, I got arrested on drug charges." Princess was still bitter.

All of a sudden, she noticed all the track marks and sores on every visible part of Big Sexy's body.

"Honey, you are too much of a good-looking girl to be gettin' arrested over some damn drugs," said Big Sexy.

"Stupid bitch ratted me out." She explained to Big Sexy that the situation was much deeper. Big Sexy told her that she understood.

"You should beat that bitch with a bat every time you see that ho." Spat Big Sexy.

"Princess Franklin, you have court," spat the officer.

"Excuse me, Big Sexy, they calling me for court," said a nervous Princess.

"A'ight suga, don't give that judge no static baby. That cracka' muthafucka love throwin' the book at us colored girls."

## Chapter Sixty-Seven

Princess' heart sank when the fat cracker bastard denied her bail and adjourned her case for thirty days, suggesting that she utilize the time to adjust her attitude problem. She turned to her lawyer with a "do something" look, but Princess, coming up in the court room rolling her eyes and sucking her teeth before the judge, made it difficult to do anything.

As she was being escorted back to the cell. Princess turned to Marcus. He shook his head in disappointment.

Damn, I knew her attitude was gon' get her in trouble one day.

***** 

### *An Hour Later...*

As soon as he walked in the apartment, Marcus heard the phone ringing.

"Yo," Marcus answered, rushing over to the phone.

"Hey, Marcus," Princess said.

"Ain't no 'hey,' Princess. What the fuck was all that attitude about today? Don't you know fucking around with the judge like that, you only playing with your freedom, dummy? You could have all the attitude you want with them fucking police, but you ain't never supposed to fuck around with no judge. But I guess now you found that shit out the hard way, right?"

"Yeah, I guess you're right, but they had it in for me from the door, 'cause these cops in here already told me how it was gon' go down. That's why I had an attitude," Princess explained.

"Regardless, you don't fuck around with the nigga that holds your freedom card."

"Well, do you think he'll let me out on bail my next court date?'

"Yo, Princess, you disrespected a judge in his courtroom, so I don't know. He might make you wait it out until sentencing."

"Damn, I fucked up!"

"Yeah, that you did."

"Well, I got to go now. I'll let you know my visitors schedule as soon as I know it, a'ight. I love you!"

"A'ight, Princess. I love ya ass too, ay, keep your head up, baby girl. Shit'll be okay!"

## Chapter Sixty-Eight

Twin had just finished packing when she looked at the time and realized it was almost noon, which meant Cadillac Dave should be expecting her soon. The closer it got to noon, the more excited she became.

Twin reached for her ringing cell phone in her purse and accidentally pulled out K'Dub's chain, which she thought would be a nice gift for Cadillac Dave. She grabbed her phone and noticed the screen read BLOCKED. Normally she didn't answer blocked calls, but she wasn't going to take any chances on missing Cadillac Dave, so she answered.

"Hello?"

"Yo, why you play me like that? That was some fucked-up shit you did. You know that, right?" K'Dub said.

"What? Nigga get over it! What? You thought I wasn't gon' remember what you did to me? Well, the joke's on you, muthafucka. It was a game, nigga. You can't possibly be that dumb to think that I would fuck with you knowing that your boy is the nigga that shot me--or maybe you are.

"You act like your pussy is gold." spat K'Dub.

"You know what? It must be, because your stupid ass went hard for it this time. Unfortunately, you've been punked, muthafucka!" Twin was filled with vindication as she slammed down the hood of her phone.

"K'Dub was steaming mad. Twin might have thought this shit was over, but this time he was gonna see to it that she pushed up daisies.

Nobody gonna play me like that and live to tell it. He sat on the edge of the bed and waited for Hershey to bring him some clothes.

"Yeah bitch, you thought I was asleep when you said you had plans for me, but oh, do I have plans for your conniving, thirsty ass."

I can't believe this bitch done walked off and stole my shit, K'Dub said as she shook his head from side to side.

He then threw the hotel phone against the wall and screamed, "YOU STOLE MY SHIT BITCH. WITHOUT EVEN GIVING ME NO PUSSY!"

Meanwhile, Twin would have felt threatened if K'Dub knew where she lived, but since he didn't, fuck him. Right after she hung up on K'Dub, she called Cadillac Dave to say she was only fifteen minutes away. Twin was ready to put the Southside of Atlanta behind her and all of its drama. But moving to the other side of town was only minutes away. She still hadn't escaped the wrath that K'Dub was going to inflict upon her and little did she know, he did know where she lived.

"Fuck K'Dub," Twin said, as she flipped her middle finger out of the window and sped off into the sunset. "If you want me nigga, then get at me."

*To Be Continued...*
Hard and Ruthless 3
Coming Soon

# Submission Guideline

Submit the first three chapters of your completed manuscript to ldpsubmissions@gmail.com, subject line: Your book's title. The manuscript must be in a .doc file and sent as an attachment. Document should be in Times New Roman, double spaced and in size 12 font. Also, provide your synopsis and full contact information. If sending multiple submissions, they must each be in a separate email.

Have a story but no way to send it electronically? You can still submit to LDP/Ca$h Presents. Send in the first three chapters, written or typed, of your completed manuscript to:

**LDP: Submissions Dept**
**Po Box 944**
**Stockbridge, Ga 30281**

*DO NOT send original manuscript. Must be a duplicate.*

Provide your synopsis and a cover letter containing your full contact information.

Thanks for considering LDP and Ca$h Presents.

Von Diesel

Coming Soon from Lock Down Publications/Ca$h Presents

BOW DOWN TO MY GANGSTA

By **Ca$h**

TORN BETWEEN TWO

By **Coffee**

THE STREETS STAINED MY SOUL **II**

By **Marcellus Allen**

BLOOD OF A BOSS **VI**

SHADOWS OF THE GAME II

TRAP BASTARD II

By **Askari**

LOYAL TO THE GAME **IV**

By **T.J. & Jelissa**

IF LOVING YOU IS WRONG... **III**

By **Jelissa**

TRUE SAVAGE **VIII**

MIDNIGHT CARTEL IV

DOPE BOY MAGIC IV

CITY OF KINGZ III

By **Chris Green**

BLAST FOR ME **III**

A SAVAGE DOPEBOY III

CUTTHROAT MAFIA III

DUFFLE BAG CARTEL VI

HEARTLESS GOON VI

By **Ghost**

A HUSTLER'S DECEIT III

KILL ZONE **II**

BAE BELONGS TO ME III

A DOPE BOY'S QUEEN III

By **Aryanna**

COKE KINGS V

KING OF THE TRAP III

By **T.J. Edwards**

GORILLAZ IN THE BAY V

3X KRAZY III

**De'Kari**

THE STREETS ARE CALLING II

**Duquie Wilson**

KINGPIN KILLAZ IV

STREET KINGS III

PAID IN BLOOD III

CARTEL KILLAZ IV

DOPE GODS III

**Hood Rich**

SINS OF A HUSTLA II

**ASAD**

KINGZ OF THE GAME VI

**Playa Ray**

SLAUGHTER GANG IV

RUTHLESS HEART IV

**By Willie Slaughter**

FUK SHYT II

**By Blakk Diamond**

TRAP QUEEN

RICH $AVAGE II

**By Troublesome**

YAYO V

GHOST MOB II

# Von Diesel

**Stilloan Robinson**
CREAM III
**By Yolanda Moore**
SON OF A DOPE FIEND III
HEAVEN GOT A GHETTO II
**By Renta**
FOREVER GANGSTA II
GLOCKS ON SATIN SHEETS III
**By Adrian Dulan**
LOYALTY AIN'T PROMISED III
**By Keith Williams**
THE PRICE YOU PAY FOR LOVE III
**By Destiny Skai**
I'M NOTHING WITHOUT HIS LOVE II
SINS OF A THUG II
TO THE THUG I LOVED BEFORE II
**By Monet Dragun**
LIFE OF A SAVAGE IV
MURDA SEASON IV
GANGLAND CARTEL IV
CHI'RAQ GANGSTAS IV
KILLERS ON ELM STREET III
JACK BOYZ N DA BRONX II
A DOPEBOY'S DREAM II
By **Romell Tukes**
QUIET MONEY IV
EXTENDED CLIP III
THUG LIFE IV
By **Trai'Quan**

THE STREETS MADE ME III

By **Larry D. Wright**

IF YOU CROSS ME ONCE II

ANGEL III

By **Anthony Fields**

FRIEND OR FOE III

By **Mimi**

SAVAGE STORMS III

By **Meesha**

BLOOD ON THE MONEY III

**By J-Blunt**

THE STREETS WILL NEVER CLOSE II

**By K'ajji**

NIGHTMARES OF A HUSTLA III

**By King Dream**

IN THE ARM OF HIS BOSS

**By Jamila**

HARD AND RUTHLESS III

**By Von Diesel**

LEVELS TO THIS SHYT II

**By Ah'Million**

MOB TIES III

**By SayNoMore**

BODYMORE MURDERLAND II

**By Delmont Player**

THE LAST OF THE OGS III

**Tranay Adams**

FOR THE LOVE OF A BOSS II

**By C. D. Blue**

Von Diesel

## Available Now

RESTRAINING ORDER **I & II**

By **CA$H & Coffee**

LOVE KNOWS NO BOUNDARIES **I II & III**

By **Coffee**

RAISED AS A GOON I, II,  III & IV

BRED BY THE SLUMS I, II, III

BLAST FOR ME I & II

ROTTEN TO THE CORE I II III

A BRONX TALE I, II, III

DUFFLE BAG CARTEL I II III IV V

HEARTLESS GOON I II III IV V

A SAVAGE DOPEBOY I II

DRUG LORDS I II III

CUTTHROAT MAFIA I II

By **Ghost**

LAY IT DOWN **I & II**

LAST OF A DYING BREED I II

BLOOD STAINS OF A SHOTTA I & II III

By **Jamaica**

LOYAL TO THE GAME I II III

LIFE OF SIN I, II III

By **TJ & Jelissa**

BLOODY COMMAS I & II

SKI MASK CARTEL I  II & III

KING OF NEW YORK I II,III IV V

RISE TO POWER I II III

COKE KINGS I II III IV

BORN HEARTLESS I II III IV

KING OF THE TRAP I II

By **T.J. Edwards**

IF LOVING HIM IS WRONG…I & II

LOVE ME EVEN WHEN IT HURTS I II III

By **Jelissa**

WHEN THE STREETS CLAP BACK I & II III

THE HEART OF A SAVAGE I II III

By **Jibril Williams**

A DISTINGUISHED THUG STOLE MY HEART I II & III

LOVE SHOULDN'T HURT I II III IV

RENEGADE BOYS I II III IV

PAID IN KARMA I II III

SAVAGE STORMS I II

By **Meesha**

A GANGSTER'S CODE I &, II III

A GANGSTER'S SYN I II III

THE SAVAGE LIFE I II III

CHAINED TO THE STREETS I II III

BLOOD ON THE MONEY I II

**By J-Blunt**

PUSH IT TO THE LIMIT

By **Bre' Hayes**

BLOOD OF A BOSS **I, II, III, IV, V**

SHADOWS OF THE GAME

TRAP BASTARD

By **Askari**

THE STREETS BLEED MURDER **I, II & III**

# Von Diesel

THE HEART OF A GANGSTA I II& III

By **Jerry Jackson**

CUM FOR ME I II III IV V VI VII

An **LDP Erotica Collaboration**

BRIDE OF A HUSTLA **I II & II**

THE FETTI GIRLS **I, II& III**

CORRUPTED BY A GANGSTA I, II III, IV

BLINDED BY HIS LOVE

THE PRICE YOU PAY FOR LOVE I II

DOPE GIRL MAGIC I II III

By **Destiny Skai**

WHEN A GOOD GIRL GOES BAD

By **Adrienne**

THE COST OF LOYALTY I II III

**By Kweli**

A GANGSTER'S REVENGE **I II III & IV**

THE BOSS MAN'S DAUGHTERS I II III IV V

A SAVAGE LOVE **I & II**

BAE BELONGS TO ME I II

A HUSTLER'S DECEIT I, II, III

WHAT BAD BITCHES DO I, II, III

SOUL OF A MONSTER I II III

KILL ZONE

A DOPE BOY'S QUEEN I II

By **Aryanna**

A KINGPIN'S AMBITON

A KINGPIN'S AMBITION **II**

I MURDER FOR THE DOUGH

By **Ambitious**

TRUE SAVAGE I II III IV V VI VII

DOPE BOY MAGIC I, II, III

MIDNIGHT CARTEL I II III

CITY OF KINGZ I II

By **Chris Green**

A DOPEBOY'S PRAYER

By **Eddie "Wolf" Lee**

THE KING CARTEL **I, II & III**

By **Frank Gresham**

THESE NIGGAS AIN'T LOYAL **I, II & III**

By **Nikki Tee**

GANGSTA SHYT **I II &III**

By **CATO**

THE ULTIMATE BETRAYAL

By **Phoenix**

BOSS'N UP **I , II & III**

By **Royal Nicole**

I LOVE YOU TO DEATH

**By Destiny J**

I RIDE FOR MY HITTA

I STILL RIDE FOR MY HITTA

By **Misty Holt**

LOVE & CHASIN' PAPER

By **Qay Crockett**

TO DIE IN VAIN

SINS OF A HUSTLA

By **ASAD**

BROOKLYN HUSTLAZ

By **Boogsy Morina**

BROOKLYN ON LOCK I & II

By **Sonovia**

# Von Diesel

GANGSTA CITY

By **Teddy Duke**

A DRUG KING AND HIS DIAMOND I & II III

A DOPEMAN'S RICHES

HER MAN, MINE'S TOO I, II

CASH MONEY HO'S

THE WIFEY I USED TO BE I II

**By Nicole Goosby**

TRAPHOUSE KING **I II & III**

KINGPIN KILLAZ I II III

STREET KINGS I II

PAID IN BLOOD **I II**

CARTEL KILLAZ I II III

DOPE GODS I II

By **Hood Rich**

LIPSTICK KILLAH **I, II, III**

CRIME OF PASSION I II & III

FRIEND OR FOE I II

By **Mimi**

STEADY MOBBN' **I, II, III**

THE STREETS STAINED MY SOUL

By **Marcellus Allen**

WHO SHOT YA **I, II, III**

SON OF A DOPE FIEND I II

HEAVEN GOT A GHETTO

**Renta**

GORILLAZ IN THE BAY **I II III IV**

TEARS OF A GANGSTA I II

3X KRAZY I II

**DE'KARI**

# Hard and Ruthless 2

TRIGGADALE I II III
**Elijah R. Freeman**
GOD BLESS THE TRAPPERS I, II, III
THESE SCANDALOUS STREETS I, II, III
FEAR MY GANGSTA I, II, III IV, V
THESE STREETS DON'T LOVE NOBODY I, II
BURY ME A G I, II, III, IV, V
A GANGSTA'S EMPIRE I, II, III, IV
THE DOPEMAN'S BODYGAURD I II
THE REALEST KILLAZ I II III
THE LAST OF THE OGS I II
**Tranay Adams**
THE STREETS ARE CALLING
**Duquie Wilson**
MARRIED TO A BOSS... I II III
**By Destiny Skai & Chris Green**
KINGZ OF THE GAME I II III IV V
**Playa Ray**
SLAUGHTER GANG I II III
RUTHLESS HEART I II III
**By Willie Slaughter**
FUK SHYT
**By Blakk Diamond**
DON'T F#CK WITH MY HEART I II
**By Linnea**
ADDICTED TO THE DRAMA I II III
IN THE ARM OF HIS BOSS II
**By Jamila**
YAYO I II III IV
A SHOOTER'S AMBITION I II

# Von Diesel

**By S. Allen**

TRAP GOD I II III

RICH $AVAGE

**By Troublesome**

FOREVER GANGSTA

GLOCKS ON SATIN SHEETS I II

**By Adrian Dulan**

TOE TAGZ I II III

LEVELS TO THIS SHYT

**By Ah'Million**

KINGPIN DREAMS I II III

**By Paper Boi Rari**

CONFESSIONS OF A GANGSTA I II III

**By Nicholas Lock**

I'M NOTHING WITHOUT HIS LOVE

SINS OF A THUG

TO THE THUG I LOVED BEFORE

**By Monet Dragun**

CAUGHT UP IN THE LIFE I II III

**By Robert Baptiste**

NEW TO THE GAME I II III

MONEY, MURDER & MEMORIES I II III

By **Malik D. Rice**

LIFE OF A SAVAGE I II III

A GANGSTA'S QUR'AN I II III

MURDA SEASON I II III

GANGLAND CARTEL I II III

CHI'RAQ GANGSTAS I II III

KILLERS ON ELM STREET I II

JACK BOYZ N DA BRONX

A DOPEBOY'S DREAM

By **Romell Tukes**

LOYALTY AIN'T PROMISED I II

**By Keith Williams**

QUIET MONEY I II III

THUG LIFE I II III

EXTENDED CLIP I II

By **Trai'Quan**

THE STREETS MADE ME I II

By **Larry D. Wright**

THE ULTIMATE SACRIFICE I, II, III, IV, V, VI

KHADIFI

IF YOU CROSS ME ONCE

ANGEL I II

By **Anthony Fields**

THE LIFE OF A HOOD STAR

**By Ca$h & Rashia Wilson**

THE STREETS WILL NEVER CLOSE

**By K'ajji**

CREAM I II

**By Yolanda Moore**

NIGHTMARES OF A HUSTLA I II

**By King Dream**

CONCRETE KILLA I II

**By Kingpen**

HARD AND RUTHLESS I II

**By Von Diesel**

GHOST MOB II

**Stilloan Robinson**

Von Diesel

MOB TIES I II
**By SayNoMore**
BODYMORE MURDERLAND
**By Delmont Player**
FOR THE LOVE OF A BOSS
**By C. D. Blue**

**<u>BOOKS BY LDP'S CEO, CA$H</u>**

<u>TRUST IN NO MAN</u>

<u>TRUST IN NO MAN 2</u>

<u>TRUST IN NO MAN 3</u>

<u>BONDED BY BLOOD</u>

<u>SHORTY GOT A THUG</u>

<u>THUGS CRY</u>

<u>THUGS CRY 2</u>

<u>THUGS CRY 3</u>

<u>TRUST NO BITCH</u>

<u>TRUST NO BITCH 2</u>

<u>TRUST NO BITCH 3</u>

<u>TIL MY CASKET DROPS</u>

<u>RESTRAINING ORDER</u>

<u>RESTRAINING ORDER 2</u>

<u>IN LOVE WITH A CONVICT</u>

<u>LIFE OF A HOOD STAR</u>

Von Diesel